JUDGE
NOT

A NOVEL

ANN MILLER HOPKINS

authorHOUSE®

AuthorHouse™
1663 Liberty Drive
Bloomington, IN 47403
www.authorhouse.com
Phone: 1 (800) 839-8640

Published by AuthorHouse 12/29/2017

ISBN: 978-1-5462-2008-4 (sc)
ISBN: 978-1-5462-2007-7 (hc)
ISBN: 978-1-5462-2009-1 (e)

Library of Congress Control Number: 2017918897

Print information available on the last page.

Part I

Chapter One

"Judge not, that you be not judged." Matthew 7:1

Judging always brings out the bitch in me. It's a gene, and I have all the markers. I also read omens. Being able to read omens is not genetic, but a gift. Almost everything is a sign pointing to what is about to happen. A broken cup, the same song on two radio stations or a race horse with your daddy's name might mean something. Sometimes you have to look squint-eyed to see an omen, but it is there.

It seemed too easy to set aside this weekend to judge a small, rural beauty pageant, an offer I would normally reject. Hungry for a change, I made a watermelon festival into an omen. How desperate am I? Being forty-nine and single chipped away at my options for every weekend, but this was too smooth. Usually, a fight ending in bargaining with my editor for time to travel to a pageant, preceded accepting a request to judge.

Ida, the magazine editor's receptionist and my stand-by for keeping V, my Bernese Mountain dog, started the series of events that channeled me here.

"Our club is planning a camp-out this weekend in the North Carolina mountains, near Cashiers. There's a class on hiking with your dog. Everybody is taking a dog. Please let me have V. You know I'm like her step-mother," Ida begged in a late-night phone call.

"Of course, you can take her. She probably needs an adventure."

I envied the camaraderie in Ida's elite group of young women. It was as real as their prowess at anything they undertook. Her little circle dominated fund raiser runs, bike races and tennis tournaments. They double-slapped palms and chanted "Gotcha back, girl," when they won an event. There was more to the club, something that made it solid, but I was not sure what.

The next morning, before I could respond to the judging request letter, punctuated with white-out, Ida leaned on my desk and mentioned I had no article deadlines that week. She alone was privy to the editor's convoluted calendar. She was privy to almost everything in the magazine office. She knew when the men's room was out of paper.

As I worked on interpreting the omen of having a rare space between article deadlines, Claude Copenhaven showed up at the office, looking older and duller than my mind's eye remembered. He had a paunch and needed a haircut. I had rarely seen him since our messy divorce was final. His sudden appearance was a definite omen. He wanted something.

Ida scurried back to her receptionist desk. She made a gagging gesture behind Claude's back.

"Hello, Abby. You're looking as beautiful as ever."

"What do you want?"

"I want to buy the river cottage from you," he said, trying to appear casual.

"Not for sale," I said, sitting back down at my small desk. He had to know how much I loved that little house, shaded by a limestone bluff on the Tennessee River, sadistic bastard. I had wrapped myself in a crazy quilt on its screened porch and watched the river to stay sane while Claude and the Alabama Courts carved away twenty-five years of gathering from my life.

"I'd like the cottage to be a family place, again," he said.

Whose family, your girlfriend's?" I asked, and stacked papers to avoid eye contact. Our divorce was final in 1982. Three years later, it was still awkward to be in the same room with him.

"The girls seem to like her," he said to inflame my resentment at our grown daughters tolerating his old secretary, now significant other.

"Sarah tells me you have another dog. You always did love the big ones. Does she stay home while you work? Is she at home now?" Claude's tone was threatening. "You have to be very careful with a big dog." He was smiling, looking hard into my eyes.

"You son of a bitch, you backed over Louise in our driveway. It wasn't my fault." I swallowed tears at the mention of that sweet, old dog. Claude had not forgotten how to hurt me. "You don't have enough money to buy my river house," I said too loudly.

"I don't know, the real estate business has been very good lately." Claude was wealthy. I was not. He smiled and tried to look cool. He had never been good at it.

"Let me explain it to you. There's not that much money. Get out."

At 5:30, I closed a file with garden photos being considered for next February's issue, and walked to my car. A note on yellow paper was wedged under the windshield wiper. I smiled, remembering my college sweetheart. He had left a note on my windshield, asking me for a date after a football game. I was thrilled and kept the note until he married someone else. We women are a foolish breed.

Use good judgement. Your house is not safe.
Texas still has outlaws.

How dare Claude threaten me? was my first thought. The Texas comment was puzzling. The paper was lined, but the note was typed. I felt like Nancy Drew.

"Mind, how you do go on," I whispered and hurried home to V.

I named her Velcro as a puppy. It felt awkward to yell Velcro, so she became V. Even then, she was busy herding me, being the buffer between me and the world. That's what Bernese Mountain dogs do. Now, at three years old and one hundred pounds, she did not endure boarding happily. I was grateful for Ida.

Good omens or bad, the signs pointed me here. And here I am, judging a beauty pageant in Cottondale, Florida. I am looking hard for the thing that will change my life. Here? What's wrong with me? The beauty contestants' interviews had begun.

I flipped a glossy photo over and pulled a score sheet from a folder with a paper watermelon glued to the corner. "26th Annual Watermelon Festival, 1985" was scrawled in homemade calligraphy. I judged the young, suntanned woman next to me, just to stay in practice. My old friend Nelle Ashford and I had made her chairperson on our unceremonious arrival to Florida and she had taken it to heart.

"How they gonna hope for a winner in Houston if we don't weed 'em out down here?" Tamsey Pike, the Mississippi judge who had joined us, leaned her full bosom forward, trying to read my notes. Her dangling earrings made a tink tink that irritated me almost as much as her audible sucking on a life saver. Tamsey was only twenty-nine, but looked older. Too many disappointments and cigarettes had taken a toll on a once beautiful woman. My almost fifty-year-old face held up pretty well next to hers, I thought. But then, I don't tan my hide.

"Don't look." I whispered and slid the edge of the interview folder over the score sheet of the first contestant, Anna Livingston.

Agnes Peabody, a teenaged pageant aide, led contestant number two into a windowless room in an unused section of the North Florida Agricultural Building. Everything in the structure, built in the fifties, was some shade of green. A humming air conditioner in the wall provided background music for our interview room.

If I had been in charge of our surroundings, there would have been a tall, Chinoiserie screen behind us. Judges would have been seated in three French arm chairs behind an eight-foot carved walnut table. The contestant being interviewed across from the judges would have sat on a graceful Bergere chair. Put that chair on a Persian rug and the whole cold process in the room would have been elevated and refined, successfully fending off the hospital green of the space. But, in this pageant or my life, I was not in charge.

Our second contestant was Sylvia Zorn from LaGrange, Georgia. She entered the low-ceilinged room with a rolling runway gait. Tall and thin, she was plain. Her thick, chestnut hair was short and swept to one side. From her minimal smile and absence of anxiousness or excitement, I felt her involvement in the pageant was at the request of someone else.

She pulled her seafoam green linen jacket down over a slender sheath of the same fabric. Only pearls punctuated the long, green silhouette in the chair.

"We have family in LaGrange," Nelle began. "Do you know the Langdales?"

"Everyone knows the Langdales. They practically own LaGrange. My grandmother on my mother's side was a Langdale," Sylvia answered.

"Mine, too." Nelle was excited.

The girl was not.

"Maybe we're cousins." Nelle laughed alone and then changed the subject. "I see you are at Valdosta State. What are you studying?"

"Science. I plan to transfer to pharmacy school at Auburn." Even the small smile was gone now.

"That's wonderful," I said to raise the energy level in our dull, AC-humming room.

"My father thinks so."

"Oh, is he a pharmacist?" Work with me here, I thought.

"No. He wants me to be one."

What's the best book you've ever read?" Tamsey jumped in, using the list of suggested questions attached to our score sheets.

Nelle and I preferred our own tried and true questions.

"Really, any science fiction, *The Martian Chronicles* or anything by Ray Bradbury."

"Makes you look at your own world with new eyes, doesn't it?" Nelle interjected, more than asked. The ex-English teacher surfaced in Nelle, and I kept score. I require my brain to keep score in several categories. A game within the game keeps me from getting stupid during these interviews.

"Yes. It's like reading poetry that shows how shallow our race, our society is," Sylvia Zorn said.

Her eyes looked older than her eighteen years and somehow sad. High cheek bones and long face gave her a serious expression that begged to be photographed at close range.

"Give the audience a big smile on that stage tonight, Sylvia," Tamsey said as a dismissal.

"I'll do my best," she said and added a weak smile as an after-thought.

"I'm afraid that girl is depressed," Nelle said when the tall contestant was gone.

"We're not therapists, we're judges," Tamsey said. "We judge, not counsel."

A folding metal chair, sadistically isolated across from our long table, set the scene for our meeting with contestant number three, a pale nineteen-year-old girl with a fixed smile.

"I'm Tonya Ray," she said, looking at each of us for a sharp, timed moment, as instructed, I presumed.

Tonya, Tamsey, where did people get such names? Their mothers must have read the same grocery store romance novels.

Nelle's slow blink let me know she had registered the names as well.

Nelle Ashford had been on the beauty pageant circuit longer than almost anyone. She drove from Savannah to ask her interview questions. Her hair, skin, suit and lipstick were beige, but her questions were always colorful.

"What is your favorite color, Tonya?"

Dramatic pause, lavender lids closed in deep thought, "Ra-id," she finally responded.

"I'm blind. Describe red to me." Nelle folded her sheet and plump arms and leaned back in her chair.

Oh, how my old friend Nelle loved that question. I'd heard it from Blakely, Georgia to Birmingham, Alabama. She was all but famous for it.

Tonya's penciled eyebrows, I noted on my sheet's margin, were too close to her eyes, and gave her otherwise beautiful face a snaky look. "It's hot and bright and bulls don't like it." She laughed at her own cleverness.

Thin top lip. I jotted down this additional reptilian feature, not simply as idle criticism, but for future identification, like a cow's ear tag. OK, too crass, even for me. Pretty, Southern agriculture queens tend to blend after a while. Side notes are necessary. I doodled a long snake on the score sheet. The first of many relevant drawings.

My turn. I pride myself on posing questions in a relaxed, conversational tone. I use my fake mellow voice to seem particularly refined. I have looked refined since I was twelve, but I only mastered the voice at twenty.

I label this voice-over a latent camouflage gene. Like sweet butter spread over tart critical juices, the voice allows an interview to continue long after the girl is history.

"In ten years, if you run into an old friend who asks what you are doing, what would you like to be able to tell her?" I asked.

"That I was a model, livin' in New York, in a penthouse." She needed no time to think that one through. She blinked rapidly. I hoped she wasn't going to strike.

I read on her entry form she had taken modeling in Donaldsonville, Georgia. I wondered if she knew what a penthouse was.

"It's what's on the inside that counts," Tonya blurted.

"Did I miss a question?" Nelle whispered. Poor Nelle had no discernable bitch markers.

The girl was done, without knowing it. Nelle and I watched her eyes light on Tamsey's jewelry. The kind that only second wives have. The girl was still too young to recognize the flashy designs not worn by those who collect pieces through anniversaries and inheritances.

"What is the single best thing about your generation?" Tamsey gestured with her large hands as she spoke. Her rings caught the light and threatened to distract.

"That we are not prejudiced about people, but accept them for what they're worth. I mean if they are black or women or anything, it don't matter."

I saw Nelle cringe. The girl was doomed in the eyes of an ex-English teacher.

I added that to my teacher column tally.

"Thank you, Tonya." Tamsey's job was to dismiss when we were about to laugh, cry or throw up.

We were allowed less than five minutes between each contestant. That was enough time to share our reactions, make notes, or convince each other why a girl would or would not be able to compete with other Ag Queens around the country. We knew the polished Houston, Dallas, Memphis and Jackson girls loomed, poised and smiling, ready to compete in the big Texas pageant with our winner.

"Well, she's nothing like her pictures," Tamsey said the moment the door closed.

"She's at FSU now. That's probably a high school picture," Nelle said.

"I think it's her hair. I don't think that's the wholesome look we want. Do you?" Tamsey spoke in my direction.

She obviously had not attended the National Ag Festival, an

extravaganza on every level. I could not respond and look at Tamsey's black, patent-leather hair at the same time, so I shifted topics.

"She doesn't seem very bright. The girl we pick will have to think on her feet to promote watermelons." I laughed and Nelle laughed like a child with me. Tamsey looked blankly at us, pressing her outlined lips tightly together. She never laughed.

We looked at Tamsey, an undisguised, gaudy, second wife with diamond encrusted pinky rings. Both hands testified to her new initials.

"In case the left hand doesn't know what the right hand's doing," I had said to Nelle when we met Tamsey a few hours earlier.

Pageant director Merle Holt introduced Tamsey as a god-sent. Mississippi Beauty queens are hard to come by in North Florida.

"The girl's not a winner on the national level. Let's get off her and on with these interviews." Tamsey pulled out contestant number four's sheet to bury the hopes of number three, who was, even as we spoke, probably saying a secret prayer.

"Ladies, here is contestant number four," Agnes announced. She winked at the taller girl she introduced and then at us before she slowly closed the door. This was the closest she would ever be to a beauty pageant.

Agnes was victim to the same powerful osmosis that creates band roadies and sports volunteers, eager to clean and store equipment. Being a part of something dreams are made of seeps into the emotions of those who would otherwise only be in the audience, the wings or the sidelines.

In this little pageant, she was the link between stage and director, judges and dressing room. Her movements were busier than necessary, shuffling papers, adjusting chairs, even touching a wayward strand of hair on a future queen.

Tonight, she would hold the trophy and roses back stage. Agnes Peabody had practiced handing off the trophy in her bedroom mirror with a large Pine Sol bottle for weeks. Her real treasures, a tiara and a trophy, stolen two pageants ago, were under her bed.

What great fortune to be the next-door neighbor of the director, Merle Holt.

"I'm Daphne Lee Stone." The girl sat gracefully in the lone folding chair and crossed her ankles to one side. Her fingers were long and relaxed in her lap. I had a feeling she came to win.

Favorite novel line on the entry form: *Gone with the Wind*. Nelle and I spied it at the same time.

"Who is Margret Mitchell?" Nelle beat me to the draw.

Tamsey looked annoyed and picked a lump of mascara from her long lashes.

"She wrote *Gone with the Wind*. I wish she had lived to write more. Wouldn't you love to know what happened to Scarlet and Rhett?"

"Yes, yes I would." Tamsey came to the rescue. "You're from Albany. What's the most beautiful thing about your city?"

"I'd have to say the Flint River." She spoke softly, allowing the words to sound like a lazy stream. There was no mistaking she was Southern, but the drawl was softened around the edges with education and travel.

Daphne smiled during the interview, but not a toothy grin that makes the face hurt by the end of a pageant. Like many Southern beauties, no one feature was breathtaking, but the face and demeanor were genteel and unforgettably feminine.

Nelle poised her red pencil against her full cheek where a dimple should be. I knew what that meant. For all her beige wrappings, Nelle loved to shock someone in the hot seat.

"Suppose the judges told you privately that to win you would have to have some kind of cosmetic surgery done." Nelle watched the girl closely while she posed the question. She had gone too far. "Would you agree to a boob job?"

Was this change of life crazy? No, I knew better. Nelle had been the same all the years I had known her: Natural linen on the outside and Arabian brocade on the inside. I think I border on being the opposite.

Tamsey nudged me with her hefty thigh under the table. Her eyes demanded I stop thinking about myself and take control of my friend. Then Daphne began to respond.

"I like myself pretty well the way I am. I just wouldn't risk any change at my age." She looked directly at Tamsey, only about ten years her senior. "You know being plump used to be in style. The Greek and Roman statues of beautiful women were fat by our standards."

We all three nodded and wrote as casually as we could on her sheet.

It was hard to find much wrong with her, except that she had made three judges feel painfully like Rubens' beauties.

"How would you promote your home town to someone considering locating a big plant there?" Tamsey assumed the whole world gloried in a factory. She knew the panacea a tire manufacturer moving to her own Morehead, Mississippi had been. When Tamsey was twelve, her mother had gone to work there during a brief single and sober period of her life.

I was grateful for anything which would fend Nelle off her favorite "I am blind" interview question. This time she asked, "What are your goals?"

"My degree will qualify me to work with the hearing impaired. And since so much main streaming is going on, there'll be times I can use the signing I'm learning."

Too good to be true, I thought. Nelle beat me to the test question. She raised one thin, pale eyebrow. "Sign something for me."

With finger arches, audible slaps of one, then two straight fingers to palm and a slight gesture toward her eye, she signed. Nelle, who had roomed for a semester with a deaf girl at Agnes Scott, nodded and smiled.

"That was beautiful," Tamsey said. And it was.

When number four was dismissed, we said we looked forward to seeing her that night in the swim suit and evening gown competition. I personally hoped she had bowed legs.

"Miss Lynn Odom, ladies," the aide I had now named Tacky Ass Agnes announced in a nasal shout. I took a long look at Merle's assistant for the first time. She had wispy feathers of hair around muddy make up, which left a white border at her hair and chin line. I disliked her intrusions into our domain. She seemed to have a special interest in this one. "Don't be nervous. They won't bite."

Every word from Lynn Odom's mouth was a sincere whine. Each unsolicited reference to the First Baptist Church in Graceville was punctuated with rapid eye blinking akin to a tic. There was no blank on the score sheet for severe afflictions.

"Is your hair natural, Lynn?" Tamsey asked. She really should leave both the hair and the natural questions to someone else.

"Oh yes." My daddy would never let me touch my hair with

anything." She spoke each syllable with an accompaniment of eye blinks.

Anything but two cans of hair spray. My money is on extra hold by the look of the five-inch loops of hair which defied gravity by floating in a permanent windblown swirl below each ear.

Nelle caught us off guard. "What is your favorite color?"

"Spare me," I mouthed. I was not spared the twanging, wordy description of baby blue.

Finally, Tamsey mercifully said, "Thank you, Lynn." Just before one of us bit her.

"By the way, are you an only child?" Nelle asked. For years I have watched her systematically support her theories while interviewing unsuspecting contestants.

Come on, Nelle. All of us took child psychology, but we don't try to use it.

"Yes, I am," Lynn answered. "But I have never been spoiled like some people say about only children." She was so upset, that she could not decide whether to stand or sit, so she hovered above the metal chair like a paranoid old woman trying to use a public toilet.

Her thighs tired and she sat, even though she had been dismissed. Lynn curled her lip at the sin of siblings.

"Thank you. Our time is running short," Tamsey said and waited for the girl to rise again, but Lynn Odom remained seated.

"My mother had a miscarriage before I was born. She was lucky to get me."

"Lucky, lucky," I whispered to Nelle without moving my lips.

"That's worth at least two extra points," Nelle said pretending to add to her sheet.

Maybe I have misjudged Nelle all these years. She just might have a genetic bitch marker after all. "Thank you, Lynn." I said glaring at the well-dressed heifer who was supposed to be getting rid of these girls on time. I was hungry and irritable and wished I only had to work with Nelle.

We waited for Lynn to close the door behind her. The stringy haired aide was peeking in. "That was the worst interview I've ever had to sit through." I said, slapping contestant number six's score sheet on top.

"No ma'am, I've had so much worse." Nelle made a perfect circle with her mouth.

"In the Miss Lake Lanier pageant, a pretty brunette said her future plans were to get the hell out of Georgia the minute she graduated. Right after that old Judge Hiram Wilson asked her to tell about her favorite Georgia resort. Can you believe that?"

"Ready?" Agnes stuck her head in the door, where she had been listening. Without waiting for a reply, she ushered in Luwanna Love.

"Is that your real name?" Tamsey began.

With a name like Tamsey, how could she question anybody's name? But then, she felt authenticity of hair color was her jurisdiction, too.

"Luwanna Love, lovely alliteration," Nelle added to soften Tamsey's first question.

I counted the number of times the English teacher surfaced in Nelle. I continued to play several games within the game to keep my mind occupied. At least that's how I excused my craziness.

"Alliteration," Tamsey repeated, feeling the mild reprimand from an experienced judge.

"It's just polyester, but it's supposed to look like silk," Luwanna said.

It certainly was polyester and pink. The shoes on the huge feet were also pink, but they were plastic. Luwanna's thin, moist hair was parted in the middle and flipped back on both sides in a neat roll. An ear protruded on one side. A solid line of blue eye shadow dominated her eyes so thoroughly that it was hard to tell what color they were.

Under the humming florescent lights, her skin was a thick white to which even the candy pink dress could lend no color.

"How long have you been out of school?" I asked, noting on the only hand-written entry form in the stack that she alone was not enrolled somewhere in something.

"Two years. I work at the Piggly Wiggly. They sponsored me, since the Slocomb chamber didn't have the time to put on a pageant this year. But I really think it's because Mrs. Moody died. That's the mayor's wife. She always did the floats for the Peanut Festival and the parade and pageant and all for the Tomato Queen. You know we have the best tomatoes in Alabama." She settled herself in the folding chair she spilled over.

"The mayor owns the Pig, so sending somebody without a contest was his way of not having a gap. Mrs. Moody wouldn't have liked that," she said and patted the dress across her lap.

That explained a lot. Long silence.

The girl relaxed a little in the metal chair, letting her back round and her stomach mound a little. Her figure was quite mature for a twenty-year-old. She looked like front porch mamas on a hundred country roads, shelling peas, while their children doodle bugged in a dirt yard.

Nelle did not retreat. "Is pink your favorite color?"

Here we go again. I made a mental check mark on one of my alternate score cards.

"No, it's Mama's. I like yellow best. But I don't have nothing yellow, not to wear, I mean."

Tamsey spoke quickly to cut off another I am blind fiasco. "Do you know who Tip O'Neil is?"

Might as well get political. Even Tamsey could see there was no controversy over the girl's hair. No one would pay money for a wig with fourteen hairs on each side of a wide part.

"I've seen him on TV, a while back. Great big feller, white hair."

"Yes, that's him." Nelle suddenly seemed to feel a soft spot for this contestant whose water buffalo mother had sprawled on two auditorium seats all morning.

"Can you tell us what his capacity is?" Nelle coached.

"From the looks of him, I'd say two gallons if he can hold a ounce."

Nelle's pencil point snapped against her score sheet. No matter. How could she write anything about this interview?

"If you ran into a friend, ten years from now, what would you like to tell her you were doing?" I asked, not allowing myself the luxury of laughter until Nelle and I were alone.

"Well, accordin' to what I was doin' right then, I guess. I mean, feedin', pricin', just ridin'."

"No, I mean in general, overall life style." I was calm. After all, I was expected to be refined, logical, poised, the epitome of a well-preserved beauty queen. It's what I do.

"Then or now?" She started to scratch her head and thought better of it. There was a ray of hope.

"Then, your future plans."

Blank stare.

"When you are thirty, what do you want to be doing for a living?" I knew how to get down.

"Oh, I see what you're gettin' at. OK. I want to be playin' a part on *The Young and the Restless*. I could totally do that."

"I bet you could." The bitch in me surfaced in broad daylight. I could not help anybody that removed from the reality.

"Thank you," Tamsey pronounced the dismissal.

I looked at Nelle for our eyes to laugh together, but she was solemn. She saw something I didn't see. Maybe the same thing the big, tired mother had seen in the girl's eyes that justified spending grocery money on a pink dress and an evening gown.

"Break a leg," Nelle called softly to the gawky girl just before she closed the door to the hallway.

"Oh, no ma'am, I won't." She looked down at her bright pink heels and smiled for the first time. It was a beautiful smile. For a second, her blind optimism made me want to weep. Weep for all the unrealistic checkout girls in the world who don't know when they have no chance. They are already beaten and their eyes still sparkle.

Chapter Two

WEATHER GIRL

I remembered all the undignified, poorly funded pageants I had won in the sixties. Once, using a dirty public restroom as a dressing room, I had stood on a toilet seat to keep the hem of my dress from getting wet.

I used titles from some of those less glamorous events to apply for a TV weather girl spot on Channel 13. The weather girl on the Birmingham station was expecting a baby and needed a replacement for the summer. It was the perfect opportunity for an Auburn University junior with twelve weeks until Fall quarter. I had taken a meteorology course, but it was my map and pointer skills during the interview that cinched the job.

One problem arose. Everything at the station was live.

A more experienced beauty on staff, Fanny Flagg, encouraged me to appear on her morning talk show to get the feel of live TV. "I'll interview you as Miss Logan Martin Lake to promote the new development. It's sort of news, plus they're sponsors," she had said.

The next morning, in a royal blue dress, I looked better on camera than I did in person. Then I began to think about being live. . . about not getting hysterically tickled. Laughter has always plagued me.

"Well, Mogan Lartin Lake, I mean Lartin Mogan," I stumbled over the corrections of corrections. Like dropping a baton at half time, once you drop it, it's all over.

Fanny was funny and talented, but no help. "Is that a new wine?" she asked, laughing. I joined her laughter and could not stop.

I was fired, then re-hired, thanks to Buddy Rutledge, the station's sports director and a loyal Auburn fan.

"Last chance, girlie, nobody thinks you're funny, but you," the skinny producer warned me at seven a.m.

I began the morning broadcast by saying "Today's feather war cast." Laughing hysterically, I moved to the map. When I pointed enthusiastically to a thunder storm in the Tennessee River Valley approaching Birmingham, the thin wooden pointer broke. It had been cut in the middle and tapped back together, as a prank. The top half swung like a pendulum. I stared at the pointer, not the camera.

Then a young cameraman began to laugh and so did I. A minute on live television is a long time. I was fired.

I cleared my head of the good old days. Now was the time to stand up for my girl, my winner. In every pageant, a judge finds one girl who fits some subconscious idea of beauty. This girl must be sold to the other judges. Her secret champion insures good placement in the pageant, even if the odds, the crowd, the scores and the contest criteria are against the choice. It becomes a challenge, a power play, another game within the game. Tamsey and Nelle were vulnerable now, with a few disappointments back to back in the pitiful interview room.

I started the dance. "Of what I've seen, I like number one, the Dothan girl, Anna." I thumbed through the stack of forms seriously. "She shows the kind of class I like to see in a young girl. And she's smart, Dean's list," I added.

"Nothing about grades on my score sheet," Tamsey said. "Number One looked like a librarian to me." She evened the edges of contestant seven's sheet on top of her folder.

"It was that awful outfit that threw you." Nelle came to my aid with Anna Livingston, the first girl we had interviewed. "Who in the world would dress in a plain white blouse and a black skirt for the very first impression?"

"Unless you were interviewing at the library," Tamsey said sarcastically. "I think it just shows her personality. They all choose their own clothes for the pageant." She leaned back in her chair, fished out a gold mesh cigarette case, changed her mind and dropped it back into her huge Louis Vuitton purse. "I always wore a bright color linen suit and then a fitted gown with lots of beading." She patted the top of her pencil lifted hair.

I wanted to know what kind of swimsuit she wore to cover her wampus butt.

"Monumental ass," Nelle had whispered as we left the ladies' room behind Tamsey after breakfast. Tamsey turned and smiled. She took it as a compliment.

I got in one prejudicial remark before the bell. "Anna's a Winter, like me. We look good in black and white." I was wearing my best color, royal blue, like Anna should have. I was about to add that Tamsey should have her color analyzed, since she was also a dark- haired Winter dressed in a no-no shade of gold. Very unflattering thoughts flew away as Agnes opened the door, this time without even a warning knock.

"Contestant number seven," Agnes said, too loudly for the small space.

The prettiest, stocky girl I've ever seen entered the room with so much energy that all three of us sat straight in our chairs automatically. The smile, dotted with dimples, was real.

"I'm Jeannie Rose from Marianna." She seated herself like a graceful athlete, large thighs pressed together so that her ankles, small below rounded calves, crossed neatly. She smoothed the hem of an expensive looking, rose-colored dress, precisely the shade of her lip gloss.

"Tell us about all these majorette awards listed on your entry," Tamsey said.

"In Nationals, I took first place in military marching and then went on to win the beauty category of Miss Southern Majorette. All of the others were basically prelims to those contests." Her voice was even and low.

She was so wholesome, I wanted to pinch her cheek, to start a new pageant for her. I didn't want her to have to compete with tall, graceful girls with long legs. I had beaten out prettier girls throughout my contest years simply because of my long legs. I almost felt guilty.

Nelle wrote a note on the corner of her folder, "Wheaties cover girl".

"Now that you've graduated from high school, I know you will miss your twirling," I said and almost threw in that I had been a featured twirler in high school.

Chapter Three

ON FIRE

1963, Legion Field in Birmingham, Alabama. . . half time. . . Stadium lights went down to a glow and I twirled two fire batons. On an exceptionally high toss, I moved my left baton too close to my heavily sprayed beehive.

Fire! Fire! Tiara and all.

Lonnie Maxwell, the only male cheerleader, had stayed on the side lines to extinguish the batons at the end of the routine.

Just as I realized I was on fire, he threw a cooler of ice water on my head. The huge audience cheered. A newspaper photographer's flashes blinded me for a moment. "Front page, baby," he said proudly and continued to snap and flash from different angles.

"Son of a bitch." Lonnie said as I ran past him, my tiara still in place.

"Son of a bitch!" I replied.

At our twenty-year high school reunion, a balding Lonnie and I embraced. "Son of a bitch!" he whispered.

"Son of a bitch!" I said, as I kissed his cheek.

Jeannie's eyes crinkled at the corners at the mention of twirling. "Let me tell you my good news. Last week I found out I'll be marching with the University of Alabama Million Dollar Band." Her dimples deepened. As natural as carrying a baby on one hip, Jeannie put her left hand on her waist and swung her right arm straight up in a perfect pose. "Ta da."

The joy she radiated made me want to be eighteen again. But I had been insecure, so worried about what people thought and said. It really wouldn't do me any good to go back. Dear God, I have wasted so much of my life worrying.

Chapter Four

BACK TO BUSINESS

I gave myself a mental slap. Back to the business of judging someone else. I'm better at that.

"If you could change one physical thing about yourself, what would it be?" I asked from a list of suggested interview questions provided by the local director. I began to count the typographical errors, but interrupted myself to guess her answer.

"I would like to be taller. I always say I'm not overweight, just under tall."

The mother in Nelle surfaced. I counted it in my side stats. "My father used to tell me I couldn't be too short, because my feet always touched the ground." Nelle often used the guise of her father's wisdom and humor to mask her own sayings. His had become hers. Corny comments were OK, if they belonged to your dead father.

We laughed like a threesome, realized the error of our ways and drew back safely to our roles.

"Thank you, Jeannie." Tamsey dismissed her. I saw the first real smile on Tamsey's heavily rouged face.

"She was just adorable. I could take her home with me," Nelle said when the door was closed. She pursed her lips and made a cheek pinching gesture in the air.

Of course, she could. Jeannie would fit right in with Nelle's two daughters. Julia and Elizabeth. Like their mother, they were short, cute and full of subtle humor. Years ago, I had asked Nelle why her girls had no interest in beauty contests. "They don't need them," she had simply said.

Tamsey reined in any infatuation with contestant seven. "Wonder if her people are Rose Jewelry or Rose Brothers' Trucking."

Nelle and I shrugged and caught a thought between us. Tamsey's new husband bought and sold diamond jewelry. He could probably buy and sell us several times, but we felt no need to divide everyone into haves and have nots.

Maybe maturity gives an indifference toward the wealth of others. Maybe background provides the lack of resentment for those who danced at the country club instead of the local armory as teenagers.

We had judged before with ex-queens who grew up poor and instinctively distrusted wealth, even after they were a part of an affluent circle. A diamond pendant, a fifty-dollar hair cut or a designer gown could doom a girl to being runner-up with a judge like Tamsey in power.

"Gittin' toward the end." Tacky Ass Agnes was more obnoxious with every interruption.

"I might slam her face in the door after the last interview," I said.

Nelle closed her eyes and shook her head no. "Even as ye think it in your heart. . ."

We both laughed as Tamsey solemnly greeted number eight. The beautiful girl joined our laughter innocently before she sat down.

"Miss Faye Hightower from Clanton, Alabama," Tacky Ass Agnes announced.

Her sable hair was lush, despite its artful disarray. Her lips rhythmically moved, either chewing gum discreetly or looking sexy. I was about to decide which when she began making her nest.

She spread her full skirt of white, crinkle cotton first to one side, then to the other, until she hid the ugly folding chair. She then tucked the fabric under one knee securely. Finally, she looked at us and smiled her readiness. She was beautiful in the romantic sense of the word. Large, lazy eyes dominated a smooth face with perfect, full lips.

Faye was surrounded by a white cloud of fabric which made her the center of an old-world portrait. Someone should be taking photos to capture this moment.

Then she began to talk.

What a blessing God could have bestowed on her had he struck her dumb until the end of the pageant.

I began this time, letting my mind race on to runners-up. "If you could change one thing about yourself, Faye, what would it be?"

"My bu-utt.." The dark, resplendent eyes and perfect mouth barely moved to make butt two syllables. It didn't matter. No one could have connected her face to that voice.

Nelle had a new pencil now, whose eraser she pressed to her cheek. I assumed throughout the years that she was creating a homemade dimple, but I saw no evidence of it, yet. Of course, she still had time, she was only forty-eight.

"What exactly do you mean?" Nelle had to ask.

"I mean it's too close to the ground. My daddy says if I step off a high curb, I'll bump my butt." She pushed a shining lock of hair back from her face. Her small hands were graceful.

"What's that on your hand?" Tamsey interrupted the butt conversation by pointing. These two may have attended the same charm school.

"It's a 14-carat gold fingernail." Faye held her pointer finger aloft proudly.

"Glad it's that finger," I whispered to Nelle.

"I see you are studying cosmetology. When will you have your license?" Nelle asked.

"I'm gettin' my hours in at The Cut Above, but I can't take State Boards 'til November. I got a lotta heads to wash before then." She rearranged her nest a little.

"Don't salons have the quirkiest names?" I asked, courting participation in one of my games within the game.

No response. "Nelle, where do you have your hair done?" I tried again.

She leaned back in her chair a little. "Fringe," she said sheepishly and pushed her always-too-long bangs to one side.

No one wanted to play with salon names. I did. There was Cuttin' Up, Shear Beauty, Cut Above, Curl Up and Dye. Didn't anybody else keep score?

"Tell us briefly about your local contest in Chilton County," I said. Perhaps like Luwanna Love's Chamber of Commerce, no real pageant was held.

"We just paraded around in a kind of ring in swim suits, then in dresses to the floor. Somebody told me that a lot was judged before we got there from the photos we sent to enter. My boyfriend's a photographer and mine was real good. He's just about made a career out of photographing me." She laughed.

"I'll bet they were good," I said. Mine used to be, too, I thought, thirty years ago.

Faye was one of the two girls in the contest just under the age limit, twenty-two. That bothers me and I don't know why.

"Faye, what is your favorite color?" Nelle asked.

Who cares, I thought, disappointed by the waste of such exquisite beauty. But then, maybe it would be a waste if she were a physicist in a white lab coat. Stop it, brain! I had all but lost count of my side scores.

"White, 'cause it's pure and all." She turned her face upward to think. That face was lovely from any angle.

"I'm blind. Describe white to me." Nelle sat back, pleased with her insertion.

Tamsey and I looked at each other with deadpan eyes.

"Well, it's light and ah. . ." Faye Hightower worked on her nest again. "I never been around anybody blind and I'm not too good at describing."

"Thank you, Faye." Tamsey was obviously through with the prettiest girl in the pageant, maybe in any pageant.

When she stood at the door, she turned her face toward us. It was a present. "Can I say something?"

"Certainly," Tamsey said. She was already arranging her forms for the next contestant and hardly looked up.

"I just love your hair. Bye." And she was gone.

A young man outside the door was quickly shooed away by the security guard.

"I'm not goin' to tell you again, son. Stay away from the girls and the judges 'til after the show tonight."

"I just don't want to miss anything," The tall, young man with a worn camera bag said. "She's so beautiful. You gotta admit that. You see all the others. You have to know. Admit it."

"I'll admit I'm tired of chasing your sorry, love sick ass off the property."

We watched the security guard through the open door. He had once been handsome. His faded denim eyes were fringed with black lashes, although his hair, badly in need of a trim, was mainly gray. He wore only the top of a uniform over jeans. It was hard to take his protection seriously until he adjusted the leather gun belt and holster low on his slim hips.

Tamsey was not amused by the girl, the guard or us. "I'm surprised you two didn't ask who Margret Mitchell was. You kept her in here seven minutes." She looked at her diamond encircled Rolex.

"No favorite novel listed. Really, her address should have given a clue to her background right off the bat, Riverview Trailer Park," I said.

Tamsey's eyes narrowed for a moment, then they glossed over. She shuffled papers noisily. I knew she had a trailer park in her history, just as I knew she was a product of several husbands, a couple of step dads and a fat, chain- smoking mother. I just knew it.

It happens to me sometimes, for no apparent reason. All my life I've laughed or hummed at the wrong times. I don't hear voices, but songs. My mother tried to cope with my problem in church and other public places by pinching and wringing the inside of my upper arm. That usually did it.

"Ding dong the witch is dead. The witch is dead, the wicked witch is dead. I think I was singing the munchkin song aloud. Not sure.

Now, Agnes burst into the room without a preliminary knock or comment.

"Three more to go and we can all go eat." She tapped my stack of papers, cackled, winked in my face and did not close the door when she left.

No sense bothering Tamsey with the petty plot I began to hatch. She had not been on the circuit long enough to understand the need for occasional catharsis through humor and humiliation. The cocky aide was my target.

Chapter Five

TOO PERFECT

"I'm Candace Young, from Houston, Texas."

She was the other twenty-two-year old in the pageant. She wore a red, geometric print dress and entered our small room like a national talk show hostess. Candace Young was stunning without being beautiful. She was Atlanta or Charlotte, while some of the girls we had interviewed were still cracker towns, one step removed from feed sack dresses.

"Mind, how you do go on," I mouthed.

"Candace, are you ever called Candy?" Nelle began.

"No Ma'am. I guess I don't look like a Candy. It's never been a problem, not even as a child." Her smile was as poised as her sitting position.

"You're a long way from home. Why didn't you enter one of the Texas Ag pageants? God knows there are plenty of them." I knew why. Competition in Cottondale, Florida was not on par with any Houston based prelim contests. Smart girl, I thought.

"I'm a student in Georgia and Florida is a lot closer than Texas," the perfect blonde said without missing a beat. Being called out by a judge did not rattle her.

With her pencil, Tamsey pointed slyly to the bottom of the sheet in front of me. She interrupted my mind singing, *you must have been a beautiful baby, you must have been a beautiful child.*

"Candace, who is James Michener?" I asked, smiling.

"He wrote *Centennial, The Source, Hawaii,* a whole book shelf of historical fiction novels. You know, you feel you've had a lesson with every chapter." Candace seemed excited that we asked about Michener.

'There's a character in *Centennial* I swear is based on my boyfriend. Somehow, he was always forgiven anything. He had an Indian wife and one in New Orleans and a best friend who loved. . ."

To stem a synopsis of the novel, Nelle asked, "What is your favorite color?"

If the stately blonde across the table from us had looked away for just a moment, I would have made a gagging motion to Tamsey. But Candace was too attentive to miss a finger, no matter how subtle, in my mouth.

"Peach," she answered, cocking her smoothly coiffed head to one side.

"I am blind. Describe peach to me," Nelle closed her eyes for a moment.

"Peach is warm and soft like an Autumn sunset. A glow around the sun in the evening, when a mist is still in the air. It's a peaceful color, not loud and jarring and not faded and weak like a tired pastel." She looked at Nelle and smiled. "Can you see it now?"

"Yes, I think I can."

I am a writer. I should have loved her description. But I didn't. She was too rehearsed, too mature, too sophisticated, too glamorous, too perfect. I don't want the bitch gene in me to keep a real winner from getting to Houston. I reprimanded my tangent thoughts.

The ag pageants were important. They did not provide lofty titles to the press and public, but insiders on the Miss America and Miss USA circuits knew the big money was often in less famous venues.

The Texas pageant we were focused on had more funds to disperse than all the more prestigious beauty contests rolled into one. Wealthy sponsors provided cash awards. I once received ten thousand dollars from a cable company for two brief appearances. Large department stores, like Loveman's in Birmingham, gave fabulous wardrobes. Delta flew winners all over the world, first class. There was more at stake than met the eye.

"I see you are a senior at Emory, so I guess you're on the home stretch." Tamsey, whose monumental ass had never graced a college campus, looked down at her sheet, sounding ill at ease. "What or who has been your greatest teacher?"

Praise the Lord, a new question.

"Successful people, older people are so valuable. I learn more from watching a person who has achieved what I want out of life, than from all the books and instructors outlining how to reach my goals. It just seems so hypothetical. Does that make sense?"

It made sense, but didn't sound very Emory to me.

Tamsey was impressed. My girl, Anna Livingston, was in definite trouble.

When she was gone we huddled like a wad of school girls when a new boy walks by.

"Girls, I think we may have our winner," Tamsey said.

The door clicked. "That little bitch is still eaves dropping," I said. "Bitchette," I corrected myself.

"Never mind her," Nelle said. "Now if she's everything she seems to be, I'm OK with it. Tell me why I don't like her." Nelle worked on her artificial dimple again.

"She throws everything off," I added weakly. "She really should be in another pageant. She's certainly too sophisticated to be Watermelon Queen. But American Agriculture Queen is quite a different story. Even then, she feels fake."

Entering through the back door to qualify for a bigger pageant was not uncommon, but I still felt resentment.

"Yes, there's something too perfect about her for sure." Nelle said.

"For Georgia, you mean?" Tamsey knew how to put us on the defensive.

This Mississippi judge was too new to pick up on Candace's Texas Two Step.

I've seen a few Mississippi Ag queens, judged a few. Who did she think she was talking to? Now I was defensive and I'm an Alabama girl. Tamsey Pike was hovering between bitchette and bitch.

"What's wrong with you two? She even answered your stupid author question." Tamsey examined her witch red nails to avoid eye contact. "I mean who the hell would know who James Mitchell was?"

Tacky Ass Agnes saved Tamsey from my cutting response.

"Aren't we missing a contestant? What happened to Mary Ann Adkins, number ten?" I asked Agnes and shuffled folders once more. "Twelve girls on my cover sheet and score sheets, only eleven folders."

"I'm not supposed to talk about that," Agnes said and stepped back into the hall.

Chapter Six

CONTESTANT NUMBER TEN

Mary Ann Adkins was the state champion fast pitch softball player from Fairhope, Alabama. She was one of four sisters and the daughter of a beautiful mother who had been the Pride of Mobile, Homecoming Queen and Maid of Cotton.

"One of ya'll is going to be in one pageant, one time for your mother. I've been to every swim meet, softball tournament, basketball game and tennis match in the Southeast. Just do one thing for me." Lanie Adkins addressed her teenaged daughters sitting on stools at the kitchen island. "I want to see somebody with a number on an evening gown, instead of a sweaty jersey. One time, that's all I ask."

The four were tall, lean athletes with blonde hair, blue eyes and a sprinkle of gold freckles. Like their father, they played sports for the joy of being strong and fast. The girls had always run when they could have walked. They were naturals their father had said.

Mother and three sisters looked at Mary Ann. She was sensitive about being beautiful in a house devoid of make-up, a house piled high with sweat pants and tennis shoes. Only Mary Ann had inherited her mother's fine cheek bones, perfect nose and impossibly tiny waist. She knew how to take one for the team, for her newly widowed mother.

For the first time in a long time, she saw joy in her mother's face when the two of them walked up and down the long driveway in high heels. They walked until Mary Ann's stride was smooth and confident. It took four two-hour sessions.

After the first half hour, the sisters squinted and stopped nudging each other. They watched their mother's first pleasant distraction since their father's death. The sisters' usual playful, insulting chatter was hushed.

When Mary Ann gave in to a salon visit for a hair style and make-up, (carefully removed before softball practice) she was transformed. Mother, sisters and coach were awe-struck.

"Don't look at the price tags," Lanie Adkins said when she and a bored Mary Ann were in a prom and bridal shop in Mobile. "We are going to get the most beautiful dress here. "

"What color?" Mary Ann asked, as though it mattered to her.

"Why, white, Honey. A blonde wins in white." She squeezed her daughter's hand and giggled for both of them.

"Ooooh, Cinderella," Alison said when Mary Ann showed her the white, beaded gown.

"Save it and we'll all take turns getting married in it." Lucy, the youngest teased, then ran upstairs with the dress to show their sister, Annie.

"Don't get that dress dirty, or try it on. I mean it, girls!" Lanie Adkins was smiling, even while yelling up the staircase.

Mary Ann fell on the couch, next to her older sister. "Give me a break, Ali. You can't imagine how bad that shop was. Three women wearing way too much perfume had to come inside a little dressing room to decide on a strapless bra for me. Then I had to try on pairs and pairs of high heels to mark how long the hem should be. They all discussed it for twenty minutes. Mama was right there with them." The sisters watched TV. She loved Alison more than anyone, even her mother. She and Alison were always on the same page.

"I'm doing this for Mama, then she can let it go," she explained. She put her head in Ali's lap and let her hair be stroked like a sad child. Mary Ann closed her eyes.

"It's OK, girlfriend. I'll cut you all the slack you need. You can't help being beautiful. It's Mama's fault," Alison said.

On Wednesday, before the drive to the Watermelon Festival Pageant, Fair Hope's team was scheduled to pitch against Birmingham's Woodlawn High School.

"Mama, please let her go," Her younger sisters Lucy and Annie pleaded on her behalf. "She's never missed a game."

"This is her time to shine," Lanie said to Coach Johnson.

"Her pitching is her time to shine, too, Mrs. Adkins," her coach had said in a late-night phone call. "She's the most talented pitcher I've ever coached. Mary Ann is a natural."

On Wednesday morning, Fairhope's team bus skidded off the rainy highway to avoid a tractor trailer truck. The school bus over turned. Mary Ann and a close friend and team mate were killed. A beautiful athlete and her mother's joy were gone forever.

Alison burned the white evening gown in the front yard. No one tried to stop her.

Chapter Seven

KAT COOLEY

Agnes entered the arena a little more tentatively with a long-haired brunette in five-inch high heels. "Katherine Cooley," was all Agnes said before scurrying from the room.

The contestant wore a black dress which fell below her calves. Long tight sleeves made the dress dramatic, glamorous in a rock star sort of way, not to mention hot.

"I'm Katherine Cooley, but everybody calls me Kat. I'm from Mexico Beach, Florida, but I don't sound like it. My mom's British. I lived with her 'til I was sixteen."

"Tell me the God's honest truth," Kat Cooley said. "Is it gonna freak you out if I wear my hair up tonight? I get it. I'm not judging you for judging me. Sorry, not what I meant." She laughed softly making her face more beautiful. "Another generation and all, I mean my boss loves me, but I still have to wear long sleeves at work. He can't get past my tattoos." She left out that she had run away from home in mother-daughter angst, landed in Miami and lived with a tattoo artist for almost two years.

She lifted the heavy, almost black side ponytail to reveal tendrils running up her neck like dainty, black vines. A turn of her small head showed a perfect profile and something blood red peeking through the tendrils.

Nelle dug in her purse for glasses.

My far vision is still good and I made out a red vagina. No, it had to be some kind-of Georgia O'Keefe bloom. What is wrong with me? What is wrong with her?

"Is that what it looks like?" Nelle whispered hoarsely.

"I'm afraid so," Kat said with a smile.

"How artistic." Tamsey scrambled to sound young and liberal. Her feigned acceptance misled the girl into sharing more.

Kat pushed her black knit sleeves up above her elbows. Graceful dragons and snake people intertwined, coiling around her forearms lovingly.

The three of us breathed in as one. Where was Nelle's "I am blind" question when we needed it?

I tried to cue Nelle to fill in the awkward silence. I closed my eyes. "I am blind," I hiss-whispered.

"I wish I were blind right now," Nelle said, not taking her eyes off the red vagina which seemed to look back at us.

I think the artist's intent was to make it look seductive with its open lips, but it looked like it was in pain.

Tamsey cleared her throat and looked at her folder. "You mentioned your boss. What do you do?"

I cringed to hear the answer. The only person I had ever seen with a tattoo was a retired Marine who cooked at the diner on second avenue, downtown, Birmingham.

"I work in a seafood restaurant, a big one. I was going to a junior college, but I made too much money in tips to stay in school. Now, I pretty much run the place."

"How did you decide to enter this pageant?" I asked. My mind screamed "What the hell are you doing here?"

Nelle seemed to hear my scream and patted my hand on the table. We both knew someone had badly fooled her.

"If this pageant can get me to Houston, I might be able to start my own place. I have a real twist on Mexican cuisine." She smiled at my look of surprise.

"My father was a chef. Mum can't boil water. And I'm about to talk my boss into backing me." Kat's laughter was musical.

Her boss and friend, old Frankie Simonetti, was a gambler. He bet on everything from horses to how many peppers a man could eat. He had bet her that the judges would put her in the running, if she kept everything covered. He thought she was the most beautiful young woman he had ever seen, and was appalled by her tattoos. Their mutual friend taught Kat to apply stage make up for the swim suit competition. For Kat to win her wager, she had to be kicked out of the pageant, when the judges discovered the tattoos. She won either way. Placing in this pageant gave her two to five thousand dollars. If she were sent packing, she had agreed to work another year with Frankie, but would collect ten thousand dollars severance pay and lots of used restaurant equipment.

"Do you have a favorite color, Kat?" Nelle pulled the tattered interview back into its bounds.

"Well, I was going to say red, but I've seen how you reacted to that." She flipped her long hair to cover her neck.

"In all fairness, it was not the color that set me back for a moment," Nelle said, looking directly into Kat's large, calm eyes. She saw no rancor or judgement there.

"OK, I'll say blue." She shrugged with a small smirk on her perfect face. "I plan to name my restaurant The Blue Plate."

Nelle pressed on. "I am blind. Describe blue to me."

"Here goes. When you're sad, people say you're blue. If something is rare, it happens once in a blue moon. You can be bruised black and blue or you can sing the blues. How many more do you want?" Now there was a tone of annoyance in her voice.

"Ask me something about real life and I can talk to you all day. This is just not my thing."

She looked at Tamsey. "Am I out before I start?" she asked sincerely.

"Nooo," Tamsey quickly answered. She lied. All in the room knew it.

"Thank you, Katherine," Tamsey said formally. Her tone implied, "Don't call us, we'll call you."

And now the last of the interviews and the hope of lunch at Miss Edna's.

Gloria Byrd was next. She was the youngest of all the contestants. I could conjure up no more perfect parallel to the child than a pink eyed, white bunny. In the right light, her beauty would have been ethereal, fairy-like. We were not in that light.

According to her entry form, her major claim to fame was being voted Most Talkative in her senior class. We discovered the title was well deserved.

"I saw a roach in the girls' bathroom here and almost died. I just hate roaches. The whole time I was reading *Wuthering Heights*, I thought the title was misspelled."

She really didn't need us. She interviewed herself, probably as well as we could have while still mulling over Candace Young.

Nelle, old pro that she was, tried to go through the motions. She guided the albino bunny girl to tell about her home town, Mt Dora, Florida. Finally, "Would you consider plastic surgery of any sort If the judges assured you of winning at the National level?" Nelle asked.

"No, I guess not," she finally said. "But I might change my mind if a doctor or somebody like that explained it to me just right," She giggled.

One more minute of that incessant laughter in a small, closed room and I could explain it to her just right, with Nelle's ten-pound purse against her bunny-white head. Mind, how you do go on, I thought.

"Thank you, Gloria," Tamsey interrupted the girl's chatter about yucky oysters. But it really didn't seem rude.

Agnes stuck her muddy make-up face, then her body into the room. "Well, what do ya'll think?" she started to sit down.

"Agnes, is it?" Nelle may have saved her life at that moment.

Agnes walked toward the table.

"Out," Nelle said.

"Huh?" She stopped in mid-air, above the metal chair she had pulled noisily across the floor to sit near our score sheets.

"Out. We have work to do and need total privacy." Nelle did not look up from her folder.

"But Mrs. Holt said I should get the interview sheets before she goes to lunch." Agnes made no move toward the door.

"I'll get the scores to her." Tamsey stood powerfully over the girl. The shoulder pads in her gold, silk blouse magnified her bulk regally.

"Ya'll let me know if you need anything. A Coke." She was backing toward the door as she spoke. "We got diet Coke." She looked directly at Tamsey.

"Out." Tamsey stared her down.

This time she closed the door all the way.

"Tell me why I don't like her." Nelle picked up where we left off before the cotton-white Gloria Byrd had entered our lives and score sheets.

"Because she's an ugly, presumptuous, country brat, spying for Merle Holt," I said, matter-of-factly.

"No, Abby. Shame on you. I mean Candace Young," Nelle scolded.

"OK. She's in a league all by herself here. Should she be penalized for that?" Tamsey leaned back in her chair and spread the folders like Tarot cards on the table.

"She really should be in another pageant. Maybe prelims for Miss USA," I said.

In the interest of time and hunger, I left out my old Miss USA pageant antidotes. They were good, too. I'm getting like the bumper sticker, "The older I get, the better I was."

"You've said all that before." Tamsey turned on me. Not smart. On me, always the arbitrator on odd numbered panels of misfits that pageant directors mistakenly think is insurance for fair judging. I have kept peace with clergy, ex-jocks, generals, visiting ex-queens and senile old park board chairmen.

No one ever confronted my judgement. From Miss Dog Patch, USA to National Peanut Festival, I have kept harmony for twenty years.

"Let's get something to eat and attack this thing fresh, back at the motel," I said, pressing my feisty gene back into its well-worn fence. My suggestion seemed to be a relief to both Tamsey and Nelle. They quickly stacked forms, extra pencils and red watermelon pens while they stood.

"I could use a strawberry daquiri right now," Tamsey sighed, turning off the wall air conditioner.

The quiet was wonderful. We had been straining to hear and didn't realize it. We looked down the hall to see if Tamsey's loud voice had carried to any goody-two-shoes, like Agnes, who might still be hanging around for gossip dirt on a judge or a hint of the verdict. We didn't leave fast enough. Merle Holt stood between us and Miss Edna's Café.

The pageant's director, Merle Holt, was fifty-eight and dumpy. She wore a full skirted, yellow shirtwaist dress and a printed, ever present scarf at her neck. It was her trade mark. She taught all her girls that every woman needed her own trade mark. Never change it. She had been faithful to hers, in and out of fashion, for thirty years.

"Tell me who you like." She rubbed her hands together like a chubby miser. Merle wore three rings on each hand. All six, lumped together, might have made one decent diamond ring. Once the critical juices start flowing, it's hard to turn them off.

"There are really three we like," Tamsey answered. She didn't know any better than to talk to a local director who would try to swing a judge in a New York minute.

"Four," Nelle corrected.

"Well, who are they?" Merle glanced over her shoulder to hurry our answer.

"We'd rather not say just yet," Nelle said.

"Oh, I don't mean to press you. Be glad you don't have to judge the Little Miss girls. But it makes the money for our big girls."

We turned away.

"I might just look through scores during lunch. I could be happy with most of these girls. Of course, there's one I'd give my eye teeth to have. You know what they say in the big pageants, the prettiest girl never wins. Why do you think that is?"

We moved toward the door, more rudely this time.

"You know, I took Becky Alford, last year's queen, all the way to first runner up in Houston. Boy! I worked on that girl. She was my choice from the very start. You'll see her tonight. I just wish everybody could see before and after photos of the girls I've groomed."

Nelle and I stood, looking at the ceiling, hands on hips. Only Tamsey had any visage of politeness.

"What was I sayin'?" Merle rearranged her ridiculous scarf, ending her self-important ritual with a toss over one shoulder. "Now if it's close and you have to choose between stacked in a swim suit and great personality, you know, witty and all, give me a girl with a sense of humor, you know, can think on her feet."

"We're on our way to get a bite to eat. We'll talk later." I headed for the dim hallway door to escape.

Merle hesitated before stepping fully aside. Had she known I had hoarded calories for two days to splurge at Miss Edna's, she would have jumped out of my path with more alacrity.

Merle pseudo whispered to our backs, high heels clicking on the green linoleum floor. "There's only one I really couldn't live with. That's the only reason I asked about the top few, three, four." She looked at Nelle. Tamsey might be labeled chairman, but Merle had been in the trade too long not to recognize the leader.

"Don't dare tell us," Nelle said flatly.

"Oh. I wouldn't dare. I'd be afraid I might influence you."

"Then for the love of Jesus, Mary and Joseph, let us go to lunch, woman," I said, with an exaggerated Irish brogue for my fake Catholic protest. Nelle rolled devout eyes at me.

"Sorry," I mouthed. I had gone to public schools and had no ability to feel Catholic guilt. I only pretended to be repentant when Nelle pointed out my disrespectful behavior.

"Be my guest." Merle made a clumsy flourish with her left hand.

"We are," I called over my shoulder.

I always enjoyed signing a ticket and leaving a generous tip as a pageant's guest. It was rare for a local restaurant to be worthy of gloating or gluttony, but Cottondale had Miss Edna's Café.

Chapter Eight

MISS EDNA'S CAFE

I had been to the small cottage café three times and had probably over sold it. There had been the steak and gravy over whipped, buttery potatoes visit, when I wrote an article on *Watermelon Alley,* the highway that runs through the middle of Cottondale. There was the chicken salad with sliced sweet grapes and pecans lunch last Spring on the way to Destin, Florida to meet daughters Millicent and Sarah. And on the last visit, I had fried catfish in crispy, light batter with jalapeno hush puppies and slaw made with sugar and vinegar dressing. The old café was almost on the way to Orlando.

We rode in Nelle's white station wagon. I volunteered for the back seat, trying not to appear as alpha as I felt. After a silence, Nelle became the camp director.

"Abby, tell Tamsey the story about Jim Nabors."

"Who?" Tamsey asked.

"You know, Goober on the Andy Griffith Show," Nelle prompted.

"Surprise, surprise, surprise," I said with a nasal twang. Tamsey and Nelle laughed at my excellent impersonation.

I began like an old radio someone clicked on. "Once, when I was seated at a pageant dinner next to Jim Nabors, he asked me how in the world I ended up in Pelham, Alabama judging that night. He explained how he had been railroaded by an old Alabama friend.

"After I proudly listed a string of titles, ending with Alabama's Posture Queen, he laughed that famous, nasal Gomer Pile laugh and said, "Next thing you know they'll have a Miss Athlete's Foot."

"Everyone at our table laughed. I know my face showed the sting.

"Our waitress, who had one gold and one missing front tooth, approached our long table. This unique dental feature was exposed when she opened her mouth impossibly wide in recognition of Jim.

"Let me tell you, there is some swift justice left in the world. She stared at his face and poured sweet tea until it over flowed. Both waitress and Jim Nabors reached for his tall glass at the same time, splashing sticky, cold tea onto his lap.

"He jumped, then glared at the immobile server, while all of us passed thin napkins to him."

"I'll brang you some more tea," she finally said and walked away.

"Suddenly everybody spit-laughed at once. Everybody except Jim." Sometimes justice is too slow, but sometimes it's right on time.

Miss Edna's Café was an old house in a tired section of the historic town. Inside the white house were mismatched, dark wooden tables laden with fresh vegetables. Miss Edna, square and old, like the house, held court at the antique cash register in a wide entry hall. Her faded blue apron was like the ones her six young waitresses wore, except hers was monogramed across her low, full breast, "Miss Edna."

Three Black women in white, butcher styled aprons worked in the aromatic kitchen and cooked comforting, simple dishes, as only they can. The women had been friends for almost twenty years. Their movements and short bursts of laughter flowed easily as they cooked, much like a kitchen full of cousins at a family reunion.

There were no menus, just a chalkboard with an elegantly lettered presentation of the day's fare. Peas, turnip greens, corn bread, fried okra, stewed and sliced tomatoes, tiny green butterbeans, fried chicken, ham dumplings, country fried steak and gravy, creamed new potatoes, pole beans, fried corn and sweet onions were listed. Tunnel of Fudge cake and peach cobbler were today's desserts.

"I could marry that chocolate cake," I said as we passed desserts displayed in a glass case from an old hardware store.

"I'll go ahead and rub my pie directly on my hips. That's where it'll end up, anyway," Tamsey added. She stopped suddenly. "I thought that's who I saw when the girls were registering this morning."

"Excuse me," she said, not looking at us. She walked to a small table and sat down with a handsome man in a khaki suit. She joined him so quickly, that he had time to rise only half way from his chair. He looked surprised.

They shook hands, then she touched her cheek to his and returned to us. As we were being seated in a corner with a window seat, we were served iced tea and home-made sweet pickles. I ate all the cauliflower pickles out of the small, glass dish.

Tamsey was flushed and sounded out of breath when she came to the table. She told us the man was an old friend from school. "I thought I recognized him when he was waiting at the registration desk, earlier today," she said, smiling.

Nelle and I shared a thought. The tan, blue eyed man was at least twenty years older than Tamsey, but absolutely beautiful. Hard to stop judging. We watched him leave. "Close your mouth, Tamsey," Nelle said.

I closed mine, too.

He did not look at us, but I saw a slightly embarrassed smile from his profile.

"Somehow I don't think we need to worry about being asked to judge this pageant again. I will miss this place," Nelle said.

"Speak for yourself. I was going to tell Merle Holt everything she wanted to know, if she hadn't let us beat the crowd to Miss Edna's."

"Where are those biscuits you raved about all the way over here?" Tamsey complained. She ate a lot, but did it daintily. Almost too mincingly for her bulk. Sipping tea, she held her pinky high to display her diamond initials.

At last, the steaming, towel draped biscuits, were brought out from the kitchen. I remembered the rough pyramid shape of the blue and white cloth over the stacked biscuits. The regal, old Black woman who served the warm tray was no one's server. All the blue aproned servers were energetic, smiling college girls. The old woman made and served only the biscuits, the main reason the crowd was there.

"I been makin' these for fauty years. Enjoy." It was quiet, rote litany, but every customer felt honored to be served by the same large, wrinkled hands that kneaded and shaped the dough.

"Who is the fourth girl, if you had to pick four?" I asked after eating the first biscuit of my planned gluttony.

"Who are the three?" Nelle was sly under all that motherly sweetness. I liked that about her. Perhaps she was a bitchette, if not a bitch judge, like me. No, bitchette should be reserved for eye rolling young girls who say, "Whatever," and punctuate with "like" instead of commas. I need to invent another name for Nelle. So much work for a crazy, categorizing mind to do. Maybe bitchlet.

"And why didn't anybody say a word when Merle Holt came to take the interview sheets? I mean, I have side bar comments I wouldn't let a sailor read," I said.

"And drawings," Nelle reminded me. "I don't even know what some of them were."

"You don't think she has them, do you?" Tamsey's deep voice sounded strangely nervous. Had she been scribbling, too?

"Right here." Nelle patted a green folder in her lap.

"Let's don't ruin our meal. Save all this for the room. We'll kick off our shoes and hash it out before we get under any time pressure tonight. OK?" I said.

"OK." We all nodded and began buttering biscuits in earnest.

At a small table next to us, we saw Jamie. No known last name. Contestants, directors, judges and upscale dress shop owners from San Antonio to Savannah simply referred to the small, eternally young man as Jamie. He rarely stooped to ag queen level until the Houston National Pageant, but money is money, I'm told. So, between Miss Alabama, Miss USA and Miss Universe, he worked. He designed costumes and groomed contestants.

He sat very erect across from a well-dressed, weathered blonde who looked about forty-five, though her skin would have passed for a healthy sixty-year- old tennis player. Jamie's luncheon companion watched his face while he talked, illustrating his points with raised eyebrows and graceful hand gestures.

I nudged Nelle. "She must have a daughter in the pageant."

"Who?" Tamsey interrupted, too loudly for the slow hum of the room. Her mouth was full.

As I feared, Jamie looked our way and smiled knowingly. He surmised in one glance that we were the three who would continue his reputation as groomer and coach extraordinaire or dare belittle his established claims and fees by selecting an illogical winner.

His cola brown eyes judged us, squinted a nod of recognition, then returned to his paying customer. Informed of our identity, she peered at us over her coffee cup.

"He turns up everywhere," Nelle said.

"Who is he anyway?" Tamsey leaned over my biscuits at personal peril.

"Jamie. He polishes girls all over the South. I've seen him in Atlanta, Birmingham, Mobile. . ." I stopped when Nelle continued the list for Tamsey.

"OK, OK." She waved away the rest of the places. "Jamie who?"

"Just Jamie. Like Cher or. . ." Damnit. No one else came to mind.

"Looks like any other little fag to me."

Nelle and I looked at each other and then at Jamie, eating European style and balancing his fork in mid-air. Did she just say that? Did she say it out loud? I had never thought about his sexuality, only his uncanny ability to back winners.

We could hear him gently arguing against a suggested change in jewelry. He wore a lavender shirt and a thin, white leather tie, knotted below an open collar. Even in a tux, he managed a subtle air of avant garde fashion. His upsweep of layered hair, shaped carefully with mousse, formed a swag over one eye. All this created no criticism from our view point. He was an element in beauty pageant circles, and as such, was accepted, just as Nelle and I were. Tamsey was still on the outside. Staring at Jamie, her lack of a niche in our business was more evident.

Her rude comment had caught us off guard. He was totally integrated in pageant society, and could safely comment on cleavage or deliver a little reminder slap on a backside that needed to be tucked. No offense was taken. He was not masculine, but no one knew for certain that he was gay. There were no boyfriends, no flaming clothes or jewelry.

I could not recall ever having seen him with a significant other. Before I could gather what I wanted to say to Tamsey, Jamie increased the volume of his conversation. He spoke in a business-like tone carefully projected for our table. We listened without looking at him, the mother-client or each other. His cue for our attention was too clear.

"I know what experienced judges like these are looking for. You see, an Ag pageant has different criteria on this level than it does in the national arena. Deck her out like that and she'll never get to Houston, I can promise you that." His fork clicked the threat on his half empty plate.

"We hate that white gown. It washes her out something awful," The mother whispered. "Please tell her it's OK to wear the red one."

"Two other girls are wearing red. I guess their mothers thought it was appropriate for a Watermelon Festival, too." Jamie laughed a snort of contempt. "Tradition wins on this level. A white evening gown on a blonde with a runway walk as smooth as roller skates under all that flowing chiffon, and a smile as big as the Texas pageant she'll be in." Jamie hypnotized her with his description. He was good. He patted her hand which held a crumpled napkin on the varnished table top. "Excuse me, please, just a moment."

Like most people who make a living through the pageant system, Jamie knew the value of this prelim to America's Agriculture Queen. The pageant was always a big hair, big budget affair which out-did itself every August. Life sized shade trees and waterfalls were backdrops. A movie star might announce the winner, a recording artist often appeared on stage to surprise the girls during a musical number. Anything could happen.

Jamie worked his way through the crowded tables like a model. His client was sold again. She picked up the hand-written check next to her saucer. The young waitress had recognized the payor on sight, as do most serving people.

"How does he know what the other girls are wearing? We don't even know." Tamsey leaned over my food to whisper.

If her big bosom or black, horse hair touched my last biscuit, she would pay.

"It's his business," Nelle answered simply. "He probably knows what you're wearing tonight." We laughed.

Tamsey stared at his narrow back disappearing into a restroom. There was a long silence.

Her fag comment bothered me. I've never been uncomfortable with what we grew up calling sissies or with the silly men who mistakenly imitated the worst traits of women.

"Tamsey, I don't like you calling Jamie a fag. We respect each other. He has shown me kindness over the years."

"You think he'd rather be called a queen? He may like you, but the truth is, he probably wants to be you," she said, dipping into blackberry jam.

"You missed my point," I said. "I'm not a man because I spit on the ground or a woman because I cry at a sad movie. We don't have to fit traditional roles to fit." I wanted to say more, but Nelle gave me the sign to close my preachy mouth. Tamsey's attitude cut me off from telling her about Rory, my sweetest cousin, who jumped off a bridge to his death, after repeatedly being ostracized as a fag.

"Well, I wish we knew whose mother she is, anyway. How much do you think she paid him to coach her?" Tamsey addressed Nelle.

"People used to pay a flat fee, plus expenses, about five hundred for a local contest and a thousand for a bigger pageant. Someone told me Jamie gets a five-thousand-dollar retainer, plus expenses. A Miss Tennessee board member said he gets a bonus if his client is a winner or runner-up. All of that is second or third hand, so don't repeat it."

"Let's guess which girl belongs to Jamie. Who looked polished beyond her age and experience this morning?" I whispered.

"Candace, I should have known," Nelle said.

Tamsey did not seem convinced. She rolled her eyes, looked away, and sipped her iced tea with a lemon wedge still perched on the rim. I found her manners fascinating. She made no overt blunders, after all, she had been a state contestant and Mississippi groomed its beauties to some extent. But the small quirks which a common background instills cannot be erased in a few weeks of coaching. She still took toothpicks at the cash register and put on lipstick in public. Little things, perhaps, but talking with food in your mouth and serving yourself butter with your own knife indicated lack of class. And that was that.

Jamie returned to hear our conversation and follow his patron to her car. His eye framed us like a camera as he left. I felt as though we had been judged. He sensed we were not a team, that a dangerous conflict might upset the selection of an obvious winner, his girl.

Dangerous, because three women who empathize with the contestants are not predictable. It is almost as if the judges compete vicariously. The pageant becomes a symbol of self and no one can judge self with fairness.

"Tamsey, is your friend married?" Nelle asked. I knew Nelle was asking for me.

"Who? Oh, Tom. Yes. I mean, I'm not sure, it's been a long time. Maybe not." Tamsey was nervous about this man. She couldn't stop smiling, an expression not present in the interviews. Did she just arrange a little afternoon delight, right in front of us?

"Mind, how you do go on," I said or thought. It's getting hard to tell.

Although we each had a room in the small, live oak shaded motel, we designated Nelle's room as our base. I was still disappointed that the biscuits usurped the space which, in all fairness, belonged to a large serving of buttery peach cobbler. But the biscuits were worth the sacrifice. They were light in texture from soda and buttermilk and heavy in the hand from pure lard. No apologies.

I wanted to wrap one in a paper napkin to take back to my room, but I hated to completely spoil my image in front of Tamsey. There's not much glamour in a lard biscuit.

We converged on Nelle's room and followed her lead by shedding our shoes and lying down on the queen beds. A slow wash of relief eased my tired lower back and feet. The green and gold room was pleasantly dim and cool after the short drive in Nelle's white box car which never got cool in the back seat. Nelle drove with tummy pressed on steering wheel to touch the accelerator. Often, that left me, riding on the bench front seat next to her, with knees on the dash board.

Nelle sat on her bed and spread the score sheets in a semi-circle around her Buddha-crossed legs.

Chapter Nine

SILK OR SUEDE

I wanted to tell a funny story to put Tamsey at ease with us. Maybe a laugh would be a band-aid on her outsider status.

"Tell Tamsey about the man in Santa Fe," Nelle prompted me. I am always amazed how often Nelle and I are on the same page.

"My daughter and I were in Santa Fe a few years ago. She was doing an internship with an art gallery on Canyon Road." I saw in Tamsey's bored eyes that she was not impressed. She had not been to Santa Fe.

"The art opening was a cocktail party held in their fabulous gardens and gallery. A pot-bellied pig roamed between waiters serving blue cheese and walnuts on tiny endive leaves. I waited for a huge silver tray of layered cream cheese, grated egg and caviar to be passed."

"OK, I get it. It was la de ta," Tamsey said and made a circular hand gesture for hurry, wrap it up.

"Suddenly, there was the Marlborough man. The best-looking thing I have ever seen in my life. A cowboy in a tux was staring at me from across the room. I was in love. I asked a turquoise-laden artist standing next to me to stay and I nodded toward the man with a bead on me. She laughed, sipped her grapefruit-basil martini and walked away.

"My heart was pounding loud enough for the guests to hear. This is it. This is the one. He started for me with long strides. His black cowboy boots made a rhythmic tapping on the gallery's Mexican tile floor. Then he stood next to me, towering too close. I thought I would faint. I've never fainted, but this was a hell of an opportunity. He reached out and fondled the sleeve of my red dress."

"Silk, suede, silk, suede, I just couldn't decide. Sorry I was staring, but every time you turned in the light, I changed my mind. Forgive me. I'm Lloyd."

"I stared at his rugged, lined face with my mouth open. I was ready to kiss him in front of everybody. Maybe let him gently lift me off the ground as we continued kissing. I simply could not shift gears. He shrugged at my lack of introduction and walked away."

I continued to watch Tamsey. She was laughing. She looked years younger.

"The white-haired artist who had abandoned me returned. "Your gaydar is way off," she said over her glass."

"He's perfect, I whispered, looking after him."

"That was my first lesson in profiling men. You will have yours at some point. Silk, suede, silk, suede." I felt the fabric of Tamsey's sleeve between my finger and thumb.

"Stop it," she laughed and pulled away. I forgave her ignorance without speaking.

"Did ya'll see my roses?" Tamsey asked, knowing we hadn't. "I guess Jim sent them while we were at the interviews. He's always doin' things like that. And roses are so expensive now."

"I've heard that," I said. I remembered my last florist delivery. The details were too painful. Give-me-another-chance flowers from an unfaithful husband came in wave after wave, when I filed for a divorce. I took them all to the nursing home.

"I tell you he's the most thoughtful man I've ever known. All his friends say he's a different person since he married me." She sounded defensive.

I didn't care if he was a jerk or a gentleman. Tamsey Pike was not going to be a threesome with Nelle and me on the pageant circuit. A working knowledge of her was all I needed or wanted. I knew she was going to be high maintenance.

"When's the last time you got roses, Abby?" Nelle poured oil on Tamsey's glowing flame.

"Let me think. Maybe in the hospital. How old is Millicent, now?" I replied.

"She's driving, isn't she?" Nelle pretended to remind me my youngest daughter was grown.

"Dear lord, she's twenty-three," I said. "You know one of us has got to start lying about our age."

Tamsey skipped back to Jim. "When I met him, he was tom cattin' around on his wife the worst you ever heard of."

I doubted that. No need to pop her bubble with my own painful tom cattin' experiences. I'll bet his wife didn't baby sit for the other woman to give them more time. Maybe she didn't carefully pack his suitcase for a weekend rendezvous. That's another story. One too stupid to tell aloud. Stop.

"Girls, if you'll let me go to my room a minute, I have a little surprise for you. Just to help us make big decisions." I left without comments.

When I returned with an elbow knock on Nelle's door, I could tell they had been talking about me. The air had a heaviness bitches can smell.

Tamsey was curious. Nelle was loyal.

"Tanqueray, tonic, ice and limes," I said and placed the plastic tray on the small desk.

Tamsey drank her first one like water. I began mixing another. "Extra lime this time?"

"I needed that," she replied with plastic glass extended.

I poured a generous amount of gin in her glass. Nelle and I were sippers, cheap dates.

"Did you see all those little girls coming in when we were leaving?" Tamsey asked. "That's how I got started. At first, I just liked it because I got a new dress. Then everybody started makin' over me. I really liked that. Mama worked all the time and I never knew my dad. He and Mama split when I was a baby. We went to visit his sister and came home to an empty apartment. Even my baby bed was gone. Mama can still cry tellin' that story."

Tamsey held her glass out to me again.

"I hope I'm getting a good tip," I said and Nelle laughed. God love her. She always laughed at my attempts at humor. "Wait, I forgot the lime."

"It's fine," Tamsey whispered.

"You know we have to be back by seven," Nelle said. She sat nervously on the edge of her bed.

"I had trophies lined up on the T.V. Son of a bitch took every one of them."

"Your father?" I asked.

"No. I was in the second grade. Mama's boyfriend. She can still cry over all that, too."

Tamsey shook her head and let her talk return to her current husband, Jim. "Now I can't get him out of the house, except when he's on a buying trip. He buys diamonds in New York, like you would go to the grocery store and buy bread. He knows his stuff." She drained her glass. "Can you imagine carrying a briefcase with millions of dollars in loose diamonds in it?"

We said we could not imagine it.

She gave a high pitched, girlish laugh which did not match her face or body. "Yeah, marriage," she whispered.

"Yes, I remember marriage, wet towels on the bathroom floor, commode seat left up," I said to tickle Nelle, more than to annoy Tamsey.

"No ma'am. He's a lot neater than I am. He buys really nice clothes and takes care of them. We can't even share a closet." She giggled again. It didn't fit.

"Now if you tell me Diamond Jim can cook, I might take him away from you," Nelle said.

"No, but he can pick out some of the finest restaurants you've ever laid eyes on." Tamsey's vocabulary and pronunciation altered with a few gin and tonics.

"That may be even better," I said.

"Meanwhile, back at the ranch," Nelle used her Oldies radio voice. "Name your one, two and three girls, Tamsey. Let's get this show on the road."

Tamsey fished a pen out of her folder and held it. Some people need to hold a pen to think. "I say we agree on the top four and take it from there," Tamsey said.

"I've judged more pageants than I can remember." Nelle used her wise mother voice. "And I've seen some quirky results. That's why I want to make sure we're together on our number one girl, at least. If we're not, I can tell you someone that none of us would have crowned might get the roses. Almost any girl in a pageant can win if the judges start negating each other's votes." Nelle sat in the center of her bed and crossed her short legs like a yoga student.

"These scores are set up so simply, a mistake is possible." She patted the half circle of sheets around her. "It happens, and when it does, everybody wonders what happened and you go home with a knot in your stomach."

"And bitch scratched on your car," I added. "I can tell you my choices." I was proud of being able to repress my willy-nilly gene. "Number one is number one, Anna Livingston."

"The Alabama librarian?" Tamsey snorted a fake laugh. "Please."

"Number two is Candace Young, although I don't have a good feeling about her, somehow."

Tamsey rolled her big, sphinx lined eyes as I continued.

"Number three girl is Daphne Stone." I turned my back to Tamsey and ate the cold lime wedge from my empty glass.

"And if a number four were possible?" Nelle was up to something.

"The little majorette, what was her name?" I smiled when I thought of her.

"Jeannie Rose," Nelle supplied quickly. Then she pointed a pretend mic toward Tamsey, "How about you, Tamsey?"

Tamsey read from a small piece of paper to avoid eye contact and give her list a more official air. "Number one is Candace, number two is Daphne, number three is Jeannie."

"You mean to tell me Anna Livingston is not in your top three. I can't believe it. You're judging her clothes. The festival buys a wardrobe for Houston. Just judge the girl." My voice betrayed the feisty gene that sometimes finds a hole in its fence.

"And if you had to name a fourth place?" Nelle asked calmly.

Tamsey played the name like a long-held ace. "Anna, I suppose she has potential."

"Good," Nelle said. "We are almost together. That's the only good thing about a pageant with so few girls, it's easy to get the top few. If we can get the best girl for Texas, the rest will fall into place, I think. There are less problems with runners-up than the winner."

"I want to see these four in swim suits before I promise anything," I said to cover any future shifts I might make at the last minute.

"Yes, a girl's walk on that runway is critical." Tamsey imitated Nelle's professional voice. "And I don't want to hear another word about polishing later. Who knows, your librarian might wear a slinky sequin gown tonight and have a killer body in a swim suit."

"The interview is fifty percent. I don't like it, but there it is." Nelle fanned the forms with her thumb. Her short nails were painted a frosty beige. "The way we stack these scores will pretty much determine tonight's winner. Remember what I said about canceling out each other's winners, so some girl down the list goes home with the crown."

"Or the watermelon, as the case may be," I said Groucho style, flipping an imaginary cigar. Nobody laughed. I didn't mind. I was used to it.

"Okay, Miss Priss, who's your number one?" I asked Nelle.

"Okay, Miss Biscuit, I'll tell you." Nelle had almost escaped, knowing our placement to adjust her own.

"I have mixed emotions. Candace Young might do very well in Houston, unless an experienced old gal is on the panel. But I don't quite trust her. Why does a Texas girl enter in Florida? If she gets to Houston on the Watermelon Festival coat tails, she will still have the advantage of being a Texan in a Houston pageant," Nelle said. "Texans love Texans."

"She's too slick, too old, too something. So, I'm going with Jeannie, Anna and Daphne, in that order." She sounded like a Westminster Dog Show judge. Nelle folded her child-like arms across her chest and waited for an outcry.

"Jeannie Rose is precious, a dumpling, Nelle, but not a national winner. She's just too short," I said sympathetically. At five feet, ten inches tall, I didn't want to grind Jeannie's salty shortness into any of Nelle or her petite daughters' sore spots. There is a certain overflow to all criticism.

"I can't understand why ya'll can't score what you see, without digging into what if." Tamsey shook her head. "I'm not compromising my winner. Let me say that up front."

"Nobody asked you to," I said. How inexperienced at negotiating she is, I thought.

"Candace can win. You both know that. Now, you tell me why a dowdy girl who looks like a librarian appeals to your fine taste more than a gorgeous girl, handed to you on a silver platter." She tilted her head back and blew a breath like cigarette smoke in the air. "'Cause I'm gonna black ball any little country shits you put in her way. Count on it."

"Class will out, I always say." I held up my index finger primly.

"Girls, this is not a sorority chapter meeting," Nelle said softly in contrast to Tamsey's harsh, loud voice. "If we were going by the Miss Georgia format, we wouldn't be having this debate. The judges aren't allowed to confer about the contestants. And another thing, the director collects each score sheet before the next contestant enters. There's no back-tracking and adjusting." She looked at me, "Or compromising."

"And you like that?" Tamsey shouted in the small room. She poured herself another gin and tonic.

"I told you I had seen the big, smooth pageants back-fire because of rigidness and lack of communication between the judges. One judge negating another's choice, letting a lagging third girl slip in under the top two." Nelle blew her breath out slowly and eased back on the gold bedspread like cool water.

I was glad Nelle was there. Tamsey's façade, however thin, had been shed, revealing a course hell cat. How had Diamond Jim, all roses and restaurants, not seen through her? She had progressed from bitchette to bitch. I wanted to share my well documented levels, but didn't feel my audience was receptive to a bitch-labeling system just now.

"I really don't know why I don't like her. Persuade me." Nelle fluffed two pillows against the painted headboard.

"She's perfect," Tamsey said. "And if she's not real to the bone, so what? Who is?" She glared at me. "If she fooled us for six or seven minutes, she can string along another panel of judges, especially if there are men on it, and you know it."

"Then why don't I feel good about sending her?" Nelle pressed her cheek bones to relieve her ever-present sinus pain. "I want to send the right girl."

"She probably reminds you of Penny. Remember Penny?" It was rude to use an inside joke, but I was no longer concerned with being polite to Tamsey Pike.

Tamsey turned her sullen face in my direction. "Who is Penny?"

"She was a top ten finalist in Miss Georgia for three years in a row.

Every year she talked about long hours at the hospital and studying to become a surgeon. A few years later, Nelle and I walked into a gourmet meat market in Marietta and saw her picture in the manager's frame. The dates under the unflattering photo of her in a white jacket told the whole story."

Nelle and I laughed. Old patent leather hair was still angry. Okay. I knew I had to shift gears. I expected to hear a loud screeching to move from sarcasm to sweetness. "You know what I wonder?"

No one answered, so I continued. "Who is the one girl Merle Holt said she couldn't live with?" Creating a common enemy served as peace maker for a moment.

"It could very well be this Candace Young." Nelle sat up straight when she made the connection.

"I'll bet she'd tell you for a nickel," I said.

None of us had any respect for Merle's judgement or taste. We had been annoyed with her bragging and her intrusion into our space. It was difficult to look at a homely house wife turned pageant director and swallow all her alleged prowess. But now she might be the ammunition Nelle and I needed to counter Tamsey's stance.

"Call her," I said in a dare whisper to Tamsey.

"You call her." She pouted like a child. It was not becoming on her hard face.

"She likes you," I said.

"I'll dial," Nelle said and pulled Merle's card from her green watermelon pageant packet.

When Tamsey finished her short, quiet conversation with Merle Holt, we knew the verdict.

"You were right. But that just makes me want to score Candace Young higher." Tamsey flopped down on the foot of the bed." I really need, I mean want her to win tonight."

"I ought to support your girl just for spite," I said.

Tamsey had tasted a little spite and understood it. She had poured canned sardine oil in her couch an ex-husband had taken. She had mailed cruise pictures of herself and her married lover to his wife when he slapped her in public. She liked the thought so well, she smiled at me. With that generous, beautiful smile, I liked her without intending to.

"Did she say why?" Nelle, as usual, was calm and focused, always the string that pulled the tangent kites of emotion back to earth.

"Said she thought she was too old or something. Liked older men." Tamsey opened her large, penciled-lined lips to say more, but decided that was enough. We could see the motions of her brain in her face. She was too invested in this candidate. She would not be hard to deal with after all.

Merle had said much more. If nothing other than the long silences on Tamsey's part during the call, we knew there was more.

"Maybe a Sugar-Daddy," I said.

"Maybe Merle's husband," Nelle whispered.

We laughed for a minute like naughty little girls, bitchlets, bitchettes in training.

"What she said must not affect our decision tonight. You all know that. We shouldn't have asked her." Nelle looked at me. "It was really tacky of us." Nelle was all pro, suddenly, Catholic school guilt weighing in.

I sometimes kept score of the number of times I recognized her religion in her actions. How do I keep up?

We nodded agreement, but the seed had been sown and lightly covered with soil. I knew I would let Candace slip a notch or two in the swim suit or evening gown competition. At all cost, we couldn't look foolish after a pageant by crowning a beauty with babies or worse.

"By the way, did either of you notice anything out of proportion on Faye Hightower?" I arched my back for emphasis.

"You think she's had a boob job?" Nelle jumped at the bait.

"That, or she borrowed all Merle's scarves and stuffed them in her bra."

Tamsey cut short our laughter. The gin had worn off or kicked in. I couldn't judge which. "By boob job, do you mean, I mean are you trying to say when a plastic surgeon masticates the breasts?" Her attempt at being correct and precise, coupled with raised eyebrows and shoulders only increased our laughter to hysterical, breath-taking cackles.

Nelle's mascara made little brown rivulets down her cheeks. Tamsey did not move or smile.

Finally, I gasped, "Masticate means to chew." Had I been able to breathe, I would have added, "You Mississippi moron."

Tamsey remained immobile. "Well, it's masti-something and certainly not boob job. Besides, some people are well-built to start with. But I don't guess you would have thought of that."

We shook our heads no and tried to gain control. We were tired and the release was good.

"Plus, there's no rule about a girl getting a little help." Tamsey went back to her pout. She must not have pouted in front of a mirror in a long time. "Whatever she's done, she's drop-dead gorgeous."

"These girls are practically children, Tamsey." The mother in Nelle surfaced again. I tallied her score under the motherhood column for one of my private games.

"We're not talking about a little rouge and mascara here." Nelle was incensed.

"We're talking watermelons, here," I said in my best Joan Rivers imitation. No reaction.

"There's no rule, so it shouldn't be considered." Tamsey ignored me, stood and crossed her arms over an ample bosom, "not even discussed."

"Everybody talks about this surgery so lightly, like getting a tooth filled." Nelle said.

"Instead of getting your little watermelons filled." I was not entertaining Tamsey or changing her mood, so I decided to stop. No one laughs at my jokes anymore.

"Have you ever seen what they do in that operation?" Nelle curled her lip, beige under the frosted lipstick. "Phil Donahue showed a film clip where they inserted a plastic bag filled with clear jelly, right under the muscle of the breast. Then, they sewed up the bottom of the overhang, I guess you could call it." She shivered.

"The natural fold. That's where a good doctor locates the scar," Tamsey added a little too quickly.

"Thoughty of the old boys, I must say." My Cockney accent entertained no better than Groucho, Irish or Joan Rivers had. I controlled my mouth long enough to stop a plastic surgeon not ever making a three-bagger joke. Nelle and Tamsey didn't seem like baseball fans, anyway. There's little as stupid as explaining a stupid joke. I should know. No one laughs at my jokes any more. My truculent brain repeated the chorus.

"Let's get them all back and ask who wears contact lenses, or ever wore braces." Tamsey was getting ridiculous. She was really going beyond the call of duty to defend a girl she identified with. A girl not in her finalists. Maybe she's going to take on the champion of the underdog role. Dear God, I've had a little of that over the years. A judge with a plain, awkward daughter will fight you every time over an under-dog contestant.

Tamsey's voice became louder and her pronunciation sloppier as she paced. "You can't judge everything."

I tried peacemaker one more time. "And let's have a show of hands on who's had a mole removed or an abortion." I smiled at Tamsey to illustrate to the simple twit that I could be on her side. I could also stupidly list things we could not judge.

Her eyes widened, flashed anger and glared into my heart for a frightening moment. Another sore spot. I'm on a roll today. Multiple husbands, trailer parks, boob jobs, abortions. Who is this short-notice substitute?

We all reined in as if a signal had been given. Maybe it had been. Women have a protective instinct that flags the point to stop for safety. Show me otherwise and I'll show you alcohol. Now I sound like Nelle with her psychological theories.

Chapter Ten

DIAMOND JIM

A loud knock at the metal door startled us. Nelle quickly slipped on her tan pumps. Tamsey and I sat very still next to each other on the edge of the bed. We were suddenly timid.

A bearded man in cut-off jean shorts and a black tank top towered over Nelle in the open door. "Excuse me. I'm Jim Pike. I'm lookin' for my wife."

"I'm sorry. We're here with the Watermelon Festival," Nelle said anxiously. By the time the word Pike registered and overpowered the appearance of the swaggering hulk at the motel door, Tamsey was next to Nelle in the afternoon sunlight pouring into the cool recesses of Nelle's room.

"Hey, Honey." Tamsey hugged him, careful not to smudge her make-up. She turned to us. "This is my husband, Jim, I've been tellin' you about."

No, not the same one you've been telling us about and you know it. I want to see the one who's so fastidious. This must be your pet ape or body guard, dressed in some want-to-be cool teenager's cast-offs.

"Nice to meet you, Jim, I said, not daring to meet Nelle's eyes. Amazing how a natural hypocrite can rise to the occasion every time.

"Diamond Jim," Nelle said as he sat in the only chair in the room. He seemed to think his new nick name was a compliment. "If we had known you were coming," she looked at me and couldn't finish.

That was just enough to start me humming in my head, *baked a cake, baked a cake.*

"Ya'll in here together? Pretty cheap beauty contest, if that's what it is." Jim looked around the dim room and scratched his hairy thigh.

"No, we each have a room. This is just sort of a meeting room, my room." Nelle patted her bed in a me Tarzan, you Jane gesture to communicate with this out-of-place man who sat in our space.

"Oh, yeah?" He shot a squint-eyed look at his wife.

"But we stay right together the whole time," Tamsey added with a child-like urgency. "How long did it take you to drive down here? You just get here?"

"Six hours, straight." His black eyes seemed to blame her for the number of winding miles between Morehead, Mississippi and Cottondale, Florida.

"Did you take the scenic route?" I asked. Nelle and I laughed before noting Jim and Tamsey had matching senses of humor.

"I know you're tired. His nervous wife stood up from her perch on the edge of the bed. "Are we through, Nelle?"

"You're the chairman."

"Okay. I'll see ya'll at seven." She opened the door, blinding us for a moment.

I should have let her go, but I couldn't. It was too easy. "Should we make dinner reservations?" I asked sweetly when Jim's bulk blocked the doorway.

Tamsey glowered with Maybelline cat eyes.

"Naw, not for us," he said. "I saw a bar-b-que place down the road that looked pretty good. Lots of trucks in front. That's always a good sign. She's probably still dietin.'"

Not judging from lunch. I thought.

"Besides, I want to check out Rose Jewelry store while I'm here. See ya'll tonight." He shot a pistol finger at his wife and left.

"I'll walk him to his car," she said and followed him, looking quickly around the shady parking lot.

When the door closed, Nelle rolled on her bed, both hands pressed over her mouth. I butted my head on a stack of pillows.

"I can't handle this." I laughed like a crazy person.

Tamsey opened the door. We froze. "I have to go to the bathroom. I mean really go. I'll be back in a minute," she said.

"Don't you know she could just die. Bless her heart," Nelle said, straightening her face.

"Bless her heart?" I hissed.

"If she just hadn't said so much about him. I guess she thought we'd never meet him," Nelle said.

Ah, Nelle, the mother surfaced for one more point.

"Nelle, if she had never said a word, if she hadn't said she was married, he would have been pretty bad."

"Oh, not that bad, Abby." Then we laughed together like the old friends we were. We both knew a pastel polo shirt was as casual as Nelle's husband ever got.

Nelle's sweet husband Harry Wayne Ashford, Vietnam vet and golf pro, was a reserved gentleman. He never talked about the Air force or the war. But I remember one night in Myrtle Beach, after a painfully close crowning of Miss Sun Fun, Nelle and I had too many pear martinis. Martinis are like boobs. One is not enough and three is too many.

She wept recounting her gentle soul mate putting body parts into bags to return to their families in the States.

I knew so little of war, of loss, so little of being one with a husband, that I had nothing to offer but a joke to lighten the mood. Sometimes I am so stupid and shallow, I would kick my own butt, if I could reach it.

Nelle feigned a soft laugh, tissue in hand. For a long time at an ocean front table, we treaded sadness like dark, deep water. We were calm and floated in our silence without effort.

"You know why he's here, don't you?" Nelle asked, reclaiming her Buddha pose on the bed.

"No, and I don't care." I looked in the mirror and began repairing the damage my clowning had done before Tamsey returned.

"To check up on her. What's good for the goose is good for the gander," Nelle said.

"Can't you say beautiful things like you used to?" I looked at Nelle in the mirror. "When first we teach bloody instruction, or something Shakespearean, at least. I'm frankly disappointed in goose and gander."

"Oh, stop it Abby. Be serious for a minute, if you can handle that. He was trying to catch her at something. Can you imagine that? There must be a reason to drive that far to surprise your wife. I'm impressed and frightened at the same time. Do we have a role in any of this? Did you see how she looked at the man in the café? I don't want to get caught in the cross-fire."

"You think she's the only one who ever had a concerned husband?" I smoothed the arch of my eyebrow. "I had a few calls to check on my whereabouts, but they were to make sure I didn't show up at the wrong time."

"I remember all that, Abby. It was a long time ago. A long time ago." We held hands for a minute. Her short, small fingers somehow covering my long ones.

"How could I have been that dumb?" My wounds were too old to weep over, but being the laughing stock at the church, country club and car wash never completely heals. "For three years, I baby-sat his secretary's child, so they could work late. I felt so sorry for her. That's why I still feel sick after all these years. I rocked her toddler to sleep, while she rocked his world."

"Well, at least Diamond Jim's antenna's up," Nelle said and let my hand go with a firm pat.

Chapter Eleven

COUNTRY SONG

"I've got to write a country song. I could write ten biographical tunes by morning," I said. "Sometimes I think I'm living the lyrics to a really big hit."

"I keep waiting to hear one," Nelle said.

"Okay. Let's get ready to kick some swim suit butt," I said and wiped the mascara smudges away.

I took a short nap and a long shower before I returned to Nelle's room. A shower cap preserved my shoulder length hair, but it still needed a little help. I used black sequined combs to sweep the hair up and away from my face. I went through the motions of additional make-up, a stab at glamour. The older I get, the more embarrassing the string of state titles from the good old days becomes. Does the audience expect a trim beauty to stand when the judges are introduced? Are they disappointed?

I know better than anyone what an accident being a winner is. When I tried to explain the almost random selection of the most beautiful girl in a pageant, people, even my own daughters, thought I was reciting rehearsed modesty.

"Another night, another judge, another winner." I said it so often, it became a rhyme. Now I had stopped explaining. Let the world think what it liked about being a beauty queen. I may have the chorus to my first song.

"Big birthday, old gal," I whispered to the bathroom mirror.

Only Nelle knew I was on the brink of the dreaded number fifty.

She was too kind to mention the milestone which conjured visions of bags and chins to any vain woman worth her salt.

The only good thing about getting old is surprising your children with all the words to every Motown song.

I flipped off the bathroom light and sang, *and many more.*

I believe there is a survival gene. Only on the eve of this birthday has it made its presence known to me. The sensation of holding on for dear life hasn't been this strong since childbirth.

I did a few waist-bends, side to side at the foot of the bed in my room. "Time for a come-back," I said to the mirror over the low dresser. Most people can't make a come-back, because they never had a peak. That theory didn't comfort me like I thought it would.

When I stepped back into the bathroom, the fluorescent light showed the harsh edge of aging at any angle I tried. To hell with it. Maybe a little moisturizer.

There is another gene I have labeled the filter gene.

"Maybe you should write a book about all these theories," Nelle had said when I bored her with all my ideas on a long drive to Key West. It was a weak moment and I went too far. Maybe I need to keep my ideas to myself to stay clear of a psycho ward.

You can spot people who have the filter gene. They soak up the aesthetic qualities around them, regardless of background and parentage. Class rises in them, as though they mentally and physically filtered out the impurities from their lives. Like royal blood surfacing in a hovel, they sift out and absorb the best that touches them. There is always the feeling of wanting more than they've seen.

Only a few judges can identify a rare contestant with the filter gene from a simple fake. Good judges can classify a girl feigning class she has no right to. Tamsey was not qualified to judge in a situation like this. She was not a filtered person.

Candace Young was in question. She was well polished, but she had neither real class nor the filter gene. To be a national winner, a girl must have one or the other. I slipped a black lace cocktail dress over my head and added rhinestone earrings, ready. I think I still have it.

My chest felt heavy for a moment. The last time I wore this dress, Nelle told me about her youngest daughter's cancer.

Chapter Twelve

THE PACT

Nelle's girls were close in every way. They were born eighteen months apart, wore the same size clothing and shoes. Both stretched to claim a height of five feet, two inches. "I had twins a year and a half apart," Nelle often said. Julia and Elizabeth were named for Harry and Nelle's mothers.

All was right with the world, at least in the Ashford household, until Elizabeth began to have severe abdominal pain. At eighteen, she was diagnosed with uterine cancer. After a second opinion at Emory, Elizabeth had a hysterectomy. I drove to Savannah to visit Nelle a few days later. The whole family was in mourning.

Hunter McCall greeted me at the front door. "Just hanging around," he said apologetically. "I don't know what else to do."

"No one does." I patted his arm. "How is Elizabeth?"

Hunter looked down at his big hands. "Her heart is broken."

Hunter was a big, kind boy with a mop of black, curly hair and tortoise shell glasses. He had been in love with Julia since second grade. He was the tallest child in the class and she was the smallest. They became best friends, taking turns defending each other.

Hunter was brilliant and quiet. Julia was an average student and the homecoming queen. The tall, reserved boy was always at her side.

Hunter had scholastic scholarship offers from Vanderbilt, Duke, Yale and the University of Georgia. With her second ACT scores and help from an army of devoted alumni who worshipped professional golfer Harry Ashford, Julia was accepted to the University of Georgia. It was a stellar day for the science department in Athens, Georgia. Hunter McCall committed to their program the next day.

The Ashford house was his second home from the day Nelle had asked him to stay after school for cookies and milk. The McCall's lived two blocks from the Ashford's and three blocks from Savannah Elementary School. Hunter walked Julia home every day until fifth grade. Then Francine came to work in the Ashford household.

Francine knew how to do everything. She had home-made remedies for stains, fleas, and bad colds. She knew how to make surprises and after-school snacks for her girls. Only begrudgingly did she include Hunter.

"Your mama just called and said you need to go home," Francine called out to the screened porch where the children played in mild weather.

"You know the phone didn't ring," Hunter whispered to Julia.

"You stay anyway. My Barbie playhouse needs a new roof," Elizabeth pleaded.

"Miss Nelle, you got to buy more groceries. That boy eats like a grown man," Francine complained.

Then Elizabeth came to Francine for help. "Hunter has warts on his hand. The kids at school are mean and make fun of him. The boys won't let him sit at the lunch table with them. Julia and I don't have lunch periods at the same time this year. She would make those mean boys sorry, but they won't pay any attention to me."

"What you want me to do? Go down to the school house and embarrass the boy to death?" Francine said while she peeled small, red potatoes in the sink. She left a perfect red ring around each one.

"I want you to Voodoo that wart off," Elizabeth whispered.

"Where you get that kind of talk? You gonna get me fired."

"Daddy says you can do anything. You have special powers we don't understand. He saw Old Billy's boy after you took that knot off his neck. Mama says you can speak Gullah and that's what Geechees talk. She said they make New Orleans black people look tame."

"Child, hush your mouth about that kind of stuff. I was a child on

Sea Island and all my people could speak Gullah. That don't mean nothing. I was a child." Francine took a deep breath. "Then I came to Savannah one day on a big boat."

"Oh, Francine, you were a slave?" Julia began to cry.

"No, baby, it was a good day, good people to live with." Francine patted the intricate braids she had made in Julia's hair that morning.

"What about taking off that boy's neck thing?" She wiped her eyes on Francine's apron.

"That's different. I've known that family all my life. They trust me with certain matters."

"Have you ever removed a wart? I meant a big one?"

"Yes, honey, I have. It's a gift, but folks are afraid of it. Like when you said Voodoo. It ain't like that. I can just do it. That's all I can tell you." She rubbed Elizabeth's small hand on her apron. "Is that peanut butter?"

Elizabeth licked her finger and they both laughed. Peanut butter fingers was their joke.

"Brang that big boy to the kitchen and let's have a look."

Julia and Elizabeth brought Hunter to Francine. They held Hunter's big, open hand between their small ones. Francine sat on a stool near the sink.

"You afraid of Old Francine, boy?"

He looked down at her worn shoes with dark toes showing through cut openings. "Only afraid of you making me go home without your cookies." Hunter smiled and held his right hand toward her.

His palm was ringed with red and clear warts. Some were as big as pencil erasers. He could not make a fist.

"Do they hurt you?" She asked, rubbing his palm.

"Just when they bleed. I hit them on things all the time."

She cradled his hand, palm up, in both her brown hands. "Worst I've ever seen. What does your mama think about all this?"

"I don't guess she's ever looked at my hands. I try not to say anything to worry her. She worries a lot. Well, she's busy at the bank and I stay in my room a lot, when I'm not here." Hunter said the last part quietly. He lived in fear of being banished from the warmest place on earth.

Francine walked out into the back yard and returned with a handful of leaves. He could smell mint, basil and a water lily bloom from the fish pond. She rubbed them on Hunter's palm, then put a rag with warm water and baking soda on his warts. "Take 'em away, I say. Let them be gone."

The girls looked disappointed. Hunter was thrilled. "When will they be gone?" he asked.

"Tomorrow or the next day, most likely. Now git on out of here. I got cookies in the oven. If they burned, you get the crispy ones."

"I love the ones with the brown edges. I love you." He hugged her and ran out into the back yard.

"Francine, you made him cry. I never saw him cry," Elizabeth said.

"The good in that boy made him cry. Now don't you two say a word about this. I mean it."

Julia and Elizabeth hooked pinky fingers before running after Hunter.

The warts were gone in a week.

Now Francine was gone. They all missed her.

I found myself listening for her in the kitchen when I walked to the breakfast room to see Nelle. I watched Nelle weep for the first time about Elizabeth.

"It's the depression I worry about. Her physical prognosis is good, but she is sad beyond words." Nelle finished her sentence between sobs.

You know how she loves babies, baby-sits all the time. I have to stop her from kissing them in the grocery store." She put her head on her arms and rested her forehead on the round breakfast table.

"Julia slept with her last night. I think she's afraid to leave her alone. When I checked on them this morning, they were curled up like kittens taking a nap. I couldn't tell where one began and the other one ended." She laughed with tears still in her eyes.

"Let's don't cook tonight. How about me getting Chinese take-out?" I tried to lighten the heaviness in the small blue and white room. I counted the Blue Willow plates on the walls while I waited for a response.

"She doesn't eat," Nelle said, raising her head. "Hasn't eaten since she came home. Just cries. We get her to take ginger ale and a little soup.

She called for Francine in her sleep last night. I'm not sure why, but Julia got really scared. I just don't know what to do to help my baby."

The swinging door between kitchen and breakfast room in the old Tudor house opened suddenly.

"Hey. Thought we might find you two in here." It was Julia. She had a tired, swollen eyed Elizabeth in tow.

"We've figured out how to fix our problem," Julia said, pulling a chair out for Elizabeth. Julia's hand combed her sister's hair back and secured it with a long clamp from her own messy bun. Elizabeth was still in pink, floral pajamas and looked twelve years old. She smiled.

"Are you okay, baby?" Nelle ventured and reached across the table for the small hand.

"You better be worried about me, not her," Julia said, still standing behind her sister's chair. Her red sweat pants and Georgia T shirt almost matched.

Elizabeth giggled and pushed her sister's hand away a little.

"What's going on?" I finally joined in.

Nelle did not look away from her daughters' faces.

"Well, we've made a pact. When she gets ready, I'll have a baby for her."

"What?" Nelle and I said together.

"She will have our genes and we will both get to love her. Of course, I would love Elizabeth's baby anyway, so there it is. And the best part, she will owe me forever." Julia leaned her face close to her sister's. "Forever," she said slowly.

"Maybe I'll name her after Francine, instead of you," Elizabeth said in a voice raspy from crying.

"Maybe I'll have a boy. How would you like that?" Julia countered.

The four of us were laughing and crying.

Elizabeth said, "You better marry Hunter. I don't know anybody else who would go along with you, with us."

"He loves you, too," Julia said.

"I know." Elizabeth remembered Hunter sitting in the floor, repairing every doll, bicycle and motorized toy she seemed destined to break as a child. Even her science projects were a snap with him as her helper.

After a while, Julia's father delegated assembling and the more tedious problems to the mechanical prodigy that was Hunter McCall.

Yes, Julia would marry Hunter and he would do anything he was asked to keep his family happy.

Chapter Thirteen

OLD STORIES

W hen Nelle opened the door to her room for me, Tamsey was already sitting on the bottom of one of the beds.

"Is Diamond Jim joining us?" I asked.

"About eight, after the Little Miss circus is over." She spoke directly to Nelle. "Isn't he a hoot? Acts like somebody's bird doggin' me." Tamsey looked anxiously into the mirror directly across from the bed.

I looked at Tamsey's reflection for a long time. Jim Pike must have seen something I missed.

"You look wonderful, Abby," Nelle said.

I pirouetted and said thank you.

Tamsey did not comment, nor turn from her mirror image.

Nelle wore a beige chiffon chemise dress with opera length pearls. Her fine, straight hair was the same day or night. It was short with a hint of a part on one side and soft bangs.

The phone rang. Tamsey jumped, Nelle answered. She held the phone in place against her neck as if her hands were too busy.

"Harry, I'm fine. No, I was a good girl. You know I always eat well when Abby's along." She laughed softly. "No, I won't be on the road after dark. I'm leaving early Sunday morning." She changed ears and smiled during the conversation with her husband as if in his presence.

"Get the girls up for church. We've been such heathens this Summer. Thank you for calling. I love you. Bye."

"Checking up on you, eh?" I said.

We both laughed. Tamsey watched us in the mirror. Harry and Nelle had the kind of love Tamsey and I had missed. Nelle had a husband who was her best friend. No facades, no games or power struggles separated them. I could never imagine them as lovers. I must not let my mind wander too far. Once it gets started, it doesn't know when to stop. Sometimes it doesn't know how to stop.

"Anybody hungry?" I asked to stem my disobedient brain. Of course, I was. I'm always hungry. I knew I'd be famished after the pageant and I couldn't allow myself two evening meals. I never diet, precisely, just try to keep the calories and fat at bay.

"Well, I'm supposed to be dieting," Tamsey answered.

"We'll eat a light meal after the pageant, okay?" Nelle offered. "You know, you girls are good for me. You have a lot more will power than I do."

"It's not will power," I answered, smoothing the black lace at my hip line. "It's just easier to keep it than get it back." I looked at Tamsey's cleavage overflowing her gold lame dress. I was amazed that more had not escaped the size twelve dress straining to encompass a size fourteen body. "At my age," I added.

A siren came and went, leaving an audible trail which we three tried to hear after the faint whine faded into an empty lull. No one seemed willing to rekindle the Candace controversy at this point. Too much had happened in a short amount of time.

Nelle dug through her big purse. Tamsey opened her mouth, eyebrows raised for expression, then thought better of throwing a splashing comment into the still pool of silence.

My mind was busy humming *Mr. Postman, stop and see, if there's a letter, oh yeah, in your bag for me.* Okay, I'll try entertaining again. Tamsey was young enough to be amused by my sixties pageant antidotes and we needed something to get back on track.

Nelle had married young and worn make-up late, so she had skipped being a contestant, but was always interested in my stories. Now I had an audience and could be the peacemaker again. I could deliver a reprieve. My old stories were the safety valve we needed to face the three hours of togetherness in front of us. Like Macbeth's three witches casting a spell to foretell the future, we had to stir the cauldron and pluck the right one from the pot.

"The evening gowns we'll see tonight have come a long way from when I was in the middle of all this. Back then, every dress in the pageant was white, with long, white gloves, I began.

"Everybody wore white? Must have looked like a bridal show." Tamsey was hooked.

I nodded. "And we all wore our hair up for formal wear and down for swim suit competition."

They nested on the beds a little and slipped off shoes, so I continued.

"I wore my hair so bouffant and sprayed, that if you pushed one side, the other side moved." I demonstrated.

"What kind of swim suits did you have to wear?" Tamsey asked.

"One-piece maillots, solid color, usually blue, provided by the pageant," I answered, wanting to get back to hair.

"Gross," Tamsey said.

I looked at her bulk and agreed with her comment. Back to hair.

"A girl in my suite wrapped her head in toilet tissue, like a turban, every night. It worked so well, she didn't even comb it between weekly beauty shop appointments."

Tamsey rolled her eyes. I'm sure she thought I was making up the story. She was, after all, reared in a blow dryer and hot roller world.

"When I was in a pageant out in Long Beach,"

"Florida?" Tamsey interrupted.

"California. There was a red-haired girl, Miss Germany," I began again.

"What Pageant?" Tamsey stopped my flow again.

"Miss International, 1965. Poor thing couldn't speak one word of English. They taught her a few on-stage phrases using the International Phonetic Alphabet. I'll explain it to you later."

Tamsey looked at Nelle for help and got none.

"Her hair just hung there, loose. Can you imagine? In those days, you used a can of spray net a week. Her hair was copper and looked like some old German woman had stayed up all night polishing every strand. She was in technicolor and the rest of us were in black and white."

"There ought to be a separate contest for redheads, you know, like in dog shows, categories. Can a judge compare an Irish Setter with an

English Bulldog?" Nelle felt it was her turn to contribute or interrupt, so I would know she was listening.

"We felt sorry for the poor thing, long hair flowing all over the place, swinging around when she turned on the runway. Her hair had never been touched by a good American can of hair spray. We wondered what European culture was coming to."

I paused for Nelle to wipe tears of laughter from her eyes. Damn, she was the best audience.

"She won." I twirled myself with exaggerated hair swings.

I could tell that souvenir story had broken the barrier. Tamsey was not exactly rolling in the aisles, but she was smiling. That was a lot for such a highly decorated face to risk.

Now, time for gross, but true. Yes, gross might appeal to Tamsey.

"In the same pageant, there was a girl we called Lizard Woman. She drove everybody crazy. She tried to dominate everything. Had to ask questions after every dance rehearsal, just to draw attention to herself. She was willing to keep ninety-one of us on that hot stage thirty minutes after we were exhausted."

"What state?" Tamsey asked.

"Country. Monette Van Heiden, South Africa," I said and tried to start again.

"Black girl?" Tamsey asked.

Her brain made my head hurt. "White, Miss South Africa is usually white. She assumed she was at least a finalist from the first day she set foot on American soil. She got off the plane wearing a fur trimmed red suit in the middle of August. That should have told us something."

"Their seasons are reversed to ours," Nelle, the teacher, added in defense. "July is their mid-winter."

"And no one in South Africa knew that? No one knew Long Beach, California was in the nineties in August?" I replied.

"What do you mean, reversed?" Tamsey asked.

"Go on about Lizard Woman, Abby." Nelle saved me from slapping Miss Mississippi Mud.

"Why did you call her Lizard Woman?" Tamsey pressed.

"She licked her lips all the time with a tongue that was the longest, skinniest thing I've ever seen." I imitated her. Nelle cackled and Tamsey stared.

"Finally, June and I had enough of her."

"Wait. Who is June?" Now Nelle was my straight man.

"Miss California. She was Cinderella at Disney Land. That was before Disney World was built in Orlando." I added the last for Tamsey's education. Who knows, the girl might go on to play Trivial Pursuit someday.

"Anyway, we knew she got up early and exercised until she started passing horrible gas, according to her roommate, Miss Argentina. Then she made a dash for the bathroom and contaminated it for the rest of the day. I mean the maids wouldn't come in. Little Argentina had to use the bathroom next door to her room during the whole ten-day pageant."

"How did Argentina do?" Tamsey asked.

Why do you care? I thought.

"She was not in the top fifteen." How I remembered finalists from thirty years ago is beyond me.

"One morning, June and I tiptoed into Lizard Woman's room and stretched plastic wrap over her commode, then put the seat back down. Argentina crossed her heart to tell us every detail at ten o'clock rehearsal." I looked at Nelle, a stickler for detail.

"We wanted to give the girl some American religious training to take home with her." I X'ed my chest with my index finger and raised my right hand. "We also taught her pinky swear."

Miss Argentina told us Lizard Woman screamed until the hall guard came right into the bathroom with her. The smell was so bad, that the old man and the girls who had run in behind him had to put their hands over their noses and run back out." I waited for a chuckle.

"Argentina said Miss South Africa stood there flushing over and over, ignoring the huge brown pile level with the commode seat. There were brown stains all over her white, silk pajamas."

Nelle rolled back on her bed, laughing. Tamsey covered her mouth.

"For the rest of the pageant, everyone started sniffing when Miss South Africa came near. Even Miss Brazil, who never knew what was going on, went along with the joke."

"Was Miss Brazil real dumb?" Tamsey asked.

Like hair color, Tamsey should have left the IQ category alone. I controlled my sharp tongue, throttled down to bitchette, and answered.

"The powers-that-be hired a Spanish translator for her. Unfortunately, she spoke only Portuguese."

"Abby, how did you do in that pageant?" Tamsey was grateful for an opening.

"Runner-up to Miss Ohio, who then competed against the forty-one countries and did miserably."

"Who was the MC?" Tamsey probed to measure the status of a pageant that had long lost its prestige in the South. The franchise had been sold twice before collapsing.

"John Forsyth," I answered proudly. I neglected to mention those were pre-*Dynasty* days. No matter, Tamsey could not have conceived of TV before *Dynasty*, anyway.

"Anybody else famous, I mean that I would know?"

I wanted to answer in a creaky voice with "Back in the day," but thought better of the established peace.

"Have you heard of the artist Alberto Vargas? He painted pin-up girls in the forties and fifties. He was one of the judges."

"He was still alive in the sixties when you were in pageants?" Tamsey asked.

"He died in 1982."

"He was old then, but very vibrant, even sketched a couple of long-legged girls. That was his style. The figures on our trophies were from his paintings."

I swallowed the tidbit that I was one of the girls he sketched and wanted to paint later. The older I get, the better I was.

"You think having been in pageants makes you a better judge?" Tamsey used her interview voice on me.

Better than what? I wanted to snap. "Everything that makes you better, makes you a better judge of everything," I said.

"Write that down," Nelle chimed in.

"What's that supposed to mean?" Tamsey should not press the peacemaker. I can be nice just so long.

"Going to college, being married, getting divorced, having children, being beautiful, getting old."

Nelle was nodding yeses like quiet amens.

A fast shave-and-a-hair-cut-two-bits knocked loudly on our door.

Tamsey bolted, cut us off, only to barely open the door. After peering like a horror movie victim, she swung the door fully open.

Merle entered, strutting a few steps as only short-legged women can. She turned on a girlish smile, "Ya'll want to ride with me?"

"We're going to skip the drama of the Little Miss, tonight," Nelle explained, smoothing the gold bedspread.

"You'll miss a precious show. They do *Wizard of Oz* songs to warm the audience up for the big girls. Oh, the scarecrow is the cutest one. It's her little dog that plays Toto."

"We'll wait for the second feature," I said.

"Alright, then, here are the programs for tonight. Thought this might be better than me pecking out an updated agenda for you. You know my typin'." She gave a silly snort of a laugh and adjusted her scarf.

Yes, I knew her typing. My letter asking me to judge had two typos and an unforgivable subject-verb agreement error. Only her use of White-out, she cutely called boo boo ink, was worse.

"Thank you," Nelle said and took all three programs.

"Oh, do me a favor. Save two seats right behind your table for Agnes and her boyfriend. She's helped me so much." Merle started to leave, then put on brakes.

"I don't know how you did it, but I am so relieved you sent that tattooed girl packing. I promise you, her photographs and sponsor made no reference to all that mess. Agnes told me about her neck. I apologize to you all. She's the reason I had to re-type these sheets."

Nelle was upset, her voice quivered. "We didn't send her away."

"Don't worry, Nelle. She's OK. I put her on a bus myself," Merle said.

"Who are we to judge her choices? We were respectful, I thought." Nelle was rubbing her hands together.

"Who are we to judge?" Who are we to judge? Tamsey stood up. "We are the judges. We judge. And it's hard to show respect to a girl who paid money to put a permanent pussy on her neck." Tamsey said what everybody but Nelle was thinking.

Alliteration from Tamsey, I thought, but harnessed my urge to make anyone laugh. My timing has been off, lately.

The programs were manually typed, mimeographed sheets, folded in half. Tacky. Suddenly an idea hummed in my head like an old Jackie Wilson song.

"I just felt like I left ya'll with the wrong impression this morning. I don't want to hurt anybody's chances, Lord knows I've always tried to be a Christian," Merle said.

I thought she should continue trying.

"I should have shut my mouth, rather than risk being a stumbling block." Merle tugged at her pink, paisley scarf, pinned with a pink and blue rhinestone brooch.

She put her hand on the door knob, but kept talking. "I have time to straighten out any defects which might hold a really good queen back. I mean clothes, walk, weight, speech."

"I think you explained that to us earlier," Nelle said politely. Like Dr. Spock, she was friendly, but firm. "See you at the pageant." Merle was dismissed.

"She reminds me a little of Lily Ann Catlin," Tamsey said when the door was closed.

"Then I'm afraid I wouldn't like Lily Ann very much," I said.

"You don't know who she is?" Nelle said. She saw by my face that I didn't know or care.

"She's written two etiquette books and used to have a column in the Jackson paper," Nelle added. "Everybody in Mississippi . . ."

"I'm impressed." I don't know why I felt so sullen and hateful suddenly. I guess Tamsey had almost turned me against the whole state.

Now it was Tamsey's turn, or so it seemed to her. I still had stories left.

"When I was Miss Morehead, I went to Jackson for a week to rehearse for the Miss Mississippi Pageant. Miss Catlin was in charge of everything. God, she was grand. She wore that red hair up in a big bun all the time and had false eyelashes and dresses that moved, you know, flowed. She could turn and swing the best you ever saw." Tamsey's laugh was distant. "Even the orchestra stopped and started again when she clapped her hands."

Miss Lily Ann sounded like a cross between Loretta Young and Lucille Ball, but I kept my comments to myself. I didn't like being upstaged, but I didn't want to belittle Tamsey's memories. After all, I tried to be a Christian, too.

"She took me aside from all those girls and dressed me down good. First thing she told me to do was get rid of that long, country hair."

"I cried right there in front of her. I thought my hair was my crown and glory. Mama loved it. It was all the way down to my waist and coal black."

Tamsey took a cigarette from her purse and lit it. A cigarette in her mouth multiplied her coarseness.

Nelle and I curled our lips slightly at the smell, but Tamsey was too deep into her mood to notice.

"When I let her take me to the beauty shop that afternoon, she was in control. There was black hair all over the floor. I almost got sick twice." She inhaled deeply.

"Then we went to this big shopping mall and walked up and down until my legs ached. She'd get at the far end and look real casual, like she didn't know me. Then she'd nod for me to walk straight toward her. I guess I finally got it right, because she took me back to the hotel to have supper with the other contestants."

"Next morning, before I got up, she was at my door. She said let's go and don't touch your face, just take your make-up bag with you."

"I can't imagine you being so dominated, Tamsey," Nelle said, appraising Tamsey's tough exterior.

"I've always been easily led, I guess." Tamsey stirred her ashes in the glass ashtray. "By the time we got back to the Civic Center, I no more looked like a Morehead, Mississippi beauty queen than you do. If the Chamber of Commerce had seen me right then, they would have snatched me out of the line-up like an impostor."

"How did you do in the pageant?" I asked. It was only fair to return the favor. Bitchlet, Bitchette, Bitch. All done.

She blew smoke straight up. "A skinny debutante won. I was first runner-up." After ten years, there was still bitterness in her voice. "Bleached hair, no boobs and capped teeth from one ear to the other."

Tamsey was born to be a bitch. I don't think she had to go through the training stages so often provided by pushy mothers and sorority rush.

Psychologists call us alpha females, but they don't understand how to break the syndrome down as we mature. Most alphas are bitchlets, bitchettes, then bitches, with proper motivation. Observations of women around wealthier co-workers, prettier women and attractive males illustrate the distinctions. If these pageants aren't a control group worth studying, I'll take down my bitch shingle.

Chapter Fourteen

TOM ROSS

"Well girls, it's about time. The hour is nigh." Nelle stood up and brushed the lap wrinkles from her dress.

The phone rang. Tamsey sat up like a bird dog on point.

Nelle said, "Just a moment." She extended the phone toward Tamsey. "Oooh, what a deep voice."

"Me?" she mouthed, then walked between the beds to answer.

"No, it's all right. Not exactly." She pressed the phone to her breast and whispered to Nelle. "Open the curtains." We all stared out the big window, through the low, serpentine oak limbs. We were voyeurs looking in the motel office across from us.

Nelle and I watched while a tall man in a khaki suit cradled a phone in the office. There stood the beautiful man we had seen at Miss Edna's Café.

"I can't now. I mean everything's messed up. No, it's not that. Somebody came. No, not just from home. It's my husband, yes, husband. He's gone to eat right now at some bar-b-que place down the road."

Tamsey shrugged to us. We continued to stare at her, a living soap opera in Nelle's room. We could have been two housewives, watching *Days of Our Lives,* as we ironed.

"Just stay there a minute, then walk over." Tamsey replaced the receiver slowly and waved through the window.

We sat with folded hands until she finally spoke.

"He's just an old friend from Morehead. Used to be from Morehead. I knew him in school."

We didn't respond at first, but I could not stop myself from asking, "Was he your teacher?"

We wanted more. Or maybe we wanted not to be disappointed with an explanation less than lewd.

"You see how Jim is," Tamsey said.

"This is really not our business," Nelle said. "You don't need to explain."

But, like telling Merle not to tell us, her comment was wasted.

Nelle dug in her purse for something to do.

"Ya'll just go on without me and I'll meet you there before our part starts." Tamsey held her cigarette lighter with both hands.

"Oh, it's not nearly time yet." I leaned back. She would have to do better than that to make us contribute to her rendezvous.

"Look, we only have an hour." Tamsey flipped the lighter with a long thumb nail in a nervous rhythm.

"How long does it take?" I asked.

"Abby!" Nelle's tone formed a reprimand barely covered by a smile.

"I want to discuss Candace some more." I slipped off my black lace pumps.

"Damn you. Go on. Maybe I'll let her slide," Tamsey hissed through her teeth before she walked into the white tiled bathroom and slammed the door.

I knew she was lying about him. He was too new to her and she could not hide her anticipation.

Nelle and I squeezed hands, gathered up purses and shoes and hurried to Nelle's car.

The handsome man on the phone was standing just outside the office. A surge of youthful daring washed over me. I decided to meet him.

"I'll wait in the car," Nelle said, trying to sound disapproving.

When I got out of Nelle's car, Tamsey's mysterious man walked through the shade of oak branches toward me.

"Tom Ross," he said in a shockingly deep voice. He offered his hand. He was blue eyed, had a slightly crooked smile and was age appropriate. Appropriate? For what? We stood outside the old brick office and shook hands too long. I felt foolish and focused on the S shaped limbs almost touching the ground around us. The problem was his eyes. They were delft against a tan, gently lined face and looked too directly at my face.

I looked away in the general direction of Tamsey's room. "Abby Copenhaven, your friend is anxious to see you. Nice to have met you."

"You're leaving?" he asked in a bass whisper.

"I'm one of the judges, I have to."

"My daughter is a contestant."

"Please don't tell me." I couldn't stop looking at him. "Wait, I don't remember a Ross."

"Long story. Pretty dismal, except for having her." His smile made me think about kissing him, but there was a good chance he would get more than kisses in a few minutes.

Maybe a quick kiss, before anyone saw or before he could react and hurt my pride.

"Her mother left me years ago and married one of my junior law partners. Changed our daughter's last name."

Tamsey had not even known what he did for a living, lying bitch.

"The happy little family moved out of state." His voice vibrated my neck and lungs like being too close to a concert speaker. "I don't know why I'm telling you all this. My wife, ex-wife died from breast cancer last year. My daughter needed me. It's been a hard time for her, but she's a fighter, like her mother."

Were his eyes misting or squinting from the slanting sun rays?

"I would really like to see you again, he said.

"My friend is waiting for me." I backed away from Tom Ross. For the first time in years, I felt that odd, vaginal contraction that tells a woman she is vulnerable.

"Maybe we can see each other after this thing is over," he said to my back.

"Maybe." I regained control and walked too fast to Nelle's big car.

I slipped into the white Buick and took a deep breath of cold air.

"How did Tamsey get all that?"

"She said he was an old friend," Nelle said, backing out of the shady parking lot.

"Oh please. She had to tell him Jim was her husband on the phone. Then told us he sold stocks and bonds. He's a lawyer."

"You think she just picked him up down here?" Nelle asked.

"Maybe the other way around. He said he had a daughter in the pageant. Who is using who?" I was trying to justify the mismatch that was Tom and Tamsey.

"Whom," Nelle said, pulling on to the highway. "Something's fishy about all of this."

"I'll bet you Candace Young is his daughter." I said, sitting straight up in my seat. It all fell into place. "That's why Tamsey's pushing her so. I'll be damned."

"Maybe they're using each other. Nelle said.

"Is that what you call it, now? Using each other?"

Tom crossed the parking lot which separated him from Tamsey Pike.

"I think that was supposed to be the well-dressed Mr. Pike," Nelle said, watching him in the rear-view mirror.

Chapter Fifteen

THE PROGRAM

"Nelle, did you pick up one of those programs?"

"In my pocket book." She patted the over-sized, tan leather bag which accompanied denim and chiffon alike.

"Go back to the office," I said. "Hand me your program and wait just a minute. Trust me."

My brain had done it again. For a mind to have a mind of its own must be rare. I have no data on the subject and am afraid to discuss the phenomenon with anyone. Why do I want to play? I am a grown-ass woman.

"May I use your typewriter, Sir?" I asked the small, bald man behind the desk.

He spat snuff neatly into an English pea can and made me welcome to pass through the counter-top opening. There sat an old Smith-Corona portable typewriter.

I unfolded the program and carefully inserted it into the roller. The old man laughed as I pecked. He watched the curtained windows across from the office.

He would have laughed in earnest, if he had read the line I carefully inserted in the trapped white space below the list of characters in *The Wizard of Oz* skit which opened the big girl pageant.

"Toto's butthole played by Agnes Peabody, Merle Holt's assistant."

Back in the car, I waved the program like a crisp hundred-dollar bill and let Nelle take it from me. The type and the placement were so good, it took her a minute to whoop.

"Abby, you have finally lost your mind. What are you going to do with this?" She read it again, clamping her hand over her mouth.

"Why, use it to save a place for Tacky ass Agnes' boyfriend, of course."

There was a long silence.

Intrigue is not normally an element on the pageant circuit, but Tom Ross posed some questions, puzzle pieces I couldn't settle. Was insuring his daughter's win the catalyst for his affair? Did Tamsey know she was being set up? Perhaps Tamsey was the instigator of the fast fling.

Who was his daughter? Why was I so attracted to him? On the short drive to the old Agriculture Building, I asked Nelle all my rhetorical questions in a rush.

Nelle knew me too well, too long and recognized my hungry search for change, my desperate omens and ridiculous lists to entertain myself.

Was Tom Ross an omen or a turning point? Looking for lipstick, I touched the folded, yellow note in my purse. I had carefully locked my townhouse and the river cottage before leaving for Florida. V was with Ida and her friends in North Carolina. Still, I felt a little uneasy. Mind, how you do go on.

Chapter Sixteen

THE PAGEANT

Wedges of folding chairs formed a semi-circle around the stage and echoed the crowd noises when we arrived. Nelle and I took our seats facing the stage, behind a little table set for three. We watched an angry mother drag a wide-eyed, ruffle laden tot out of the cruel arena. The child was obviously guilty of soiling her panties.

"I hate these little pageants," Nelle said.

"Big time or nothing for me, I always say, kid." I glanced over my shoulder toward the main entrance for Tamsey.

"No, silly, I mean the Little Miss pageants. They make me so sad. They're just babies, so fragile. Mothers like that one screw up their priorities before the poor, little things really form any."

"Screw up?" I shamed Nelle while she searched the restless crowd with her eyes. "Is that the best an Agnes Scott graduate can do? Screw up?"

"You're getting to be a bigger snob every year, Abby. It's after seven," Nelle said. "We'll start late."

"Where is Miss Hot to Trot? I'm sure old Merle has her panties in a wad by now." I scanned the perimeter of the stage for the director, but saw, instead, the most comical human being I've ever seen on stage, screen or shopping mall. He walked down the left aisle with a rolling gait which looked like a cartoon character in slow motion.

"Nelle, turn around. You can't miss this," I whispered.

The boy stood with his huge head projected forward, saucer eyes looking for someone at the base of the runway. He put his hands into the back pockets of his jeans and rocked back and forth on his heels. Slowly he added thrusts with his wide, flat bottom, to and fro, never moving his small shoulders. Shoulders which were four feet from the lower half of his body. His lower legs might have been borrowed from a stumpy, old man.

"Nelle, that's Agnes' boyfriend."

"Who?" Nelle was still mesmerized by his rhythm.

"Agnes, Merle's aide, remember, Miss Tacky-ass?" I wanted to wave and call out Garfield. I felt sure he would answer. Nelle held my arm down.

"How do you know?" she asked.

"If he's not her boyfriend, we ought to introduce them," I said. I waved toward him and called, just loud enough for Nelle to hear, "Garfield."

"Abby, please," she was laughing as she pleaded decency.

He approached us, peering up through the bottoms of thick glasses. A yellow spotlight which some high school boys were trying to control illuminated his round face. Metamorphosis took place in North Florida at that moment. The change was more dramatic than any werewolf movie. Suddenly, he was not Garfield, but Charlie Chan. The vision struck me so quickly that I had to hum a sad song to straighten my face for an introduction. *I Went down to St James Infirmary.*

"You are Agnes' friend?" I said with great effort.

"A little more than that, if I do say so myself." He grinned and showed, no, this was too much, big, bucky-beaver teeth.

I put my head on the table in front of us, black lace arms nesting my face. Sad song, sad song, where are you? *Ain't No Sunshine When She's Gone.*

"I'm Mrs. Ashford and this is Mrs. Copenhaven." Nelle took my elbow and almost lifted me to a standing position.

"Like the snuff?" He snorted.

"No, like the Royal Danish," I answered, imitating his snorting laugh. Like his girlfriend, he did not get sarcasm. I felt no guilt, now.

"Here's your program," I said.

"Thanks," he said and plopped into a folding chair directly behind us.

"You are sooo welcome," I smiled.

"You are sooo bad," Nelle said. "Have you no shame?" She spoke out of the side of her mouth, like a Snuffy Smith cartoon.

"None, here she comes. Is he reading it? Hurry, Nelle, look." I continued to look directly at Agnes, who had changed into a blue knit dress that accented her round shoulders and wide, saddlebag hips. She had not had time to shampoo her limp hair, but had a small bun on top. I think she must have saved the hair from her brush for weeks to create it.

"He's got it open," Nelle reported.

Agnes called, "hey" to us with a disco dancer's finger to the sky gesture. She followed that with a baby bye-bye wave to her beloved Garfield Chan. "Hey, Honey," she said in five syllables. She wiggled in the seat next to him to touch hip, arm and shoulder to his.

The timing was better than an old Carol Burnette skit. His laughter exploded in her face, spitting and snorting until she stood up, hands on hips.

"What is yore problem?" she said.

He could not speak. Tears streamed down his bright pink cheeks. He pointed to the program, coughing, trying to breathe.

Agnes snatched the pale green sheet and began to read. We heard a low wail, then a furious, wounded scream.

"This is far more than I hoped for," I whispered to Nelle.

Agnes turned frantically from side to side, clutching the offending material to her flat chest.

Merle walked toward us in a mincing, little jog of hurry. Her eyebrows pushed a worry wrinkle just above her puffy nose.

"Agnes, what on earth has come over you? Everybody can see you, girl. We've got to start." Merle turned to Nelle. "Where is Tamsey? Time is important here."

Agnes brushed by her, leaving Merle's carefully placed scarf askew.

Nelle and I stood, like much of the audience, to watch the girl's frenzied race up and down, in and out and through the maze of rows. She grabbed any green paper in sight. When her arms were filled with crumpled programs, she ran to a trash can, stuffed the source of her hysteria into its depths, and started all over again. She was crazed with her chore. As single minded as a cat scratching in a litter box, no protests, no questions deterred her.

Tamsey could have entered unseen in the confusion, but the wicked hand of fate sent Agnes raging right toward the side entrance Tamsey had chosen. Two rotating, yellow spotlights caught Tamsey and Agnes in the shadows of the crowd. The lights paused on Tamsey's gold sequin dress, casting fairy glitter around her.

It's hard to separate fate and justice. Big Jim sat on an aisle seat, watching the one woman show. He waited for Tamsey to be seated next to us before he approached and hovered over our table, glaring at us all.

Tamsey paled, a miracle through fuchsia powdered cheeks. Quickly she started digging through her gold beaded purse.

"Dear Lord, does she have a gun?" Nelle gasped in my ear.

"There are not enough bullets to fix this," I answered.

Tamsey handed me an envelope and a pleading look.

I'm not proud of being able to communicate with the likes of Tamsey Pike, but I did. "I can't believe I left this cash right on your car seat. It's a miracle it was still there. Thank you. Thank you for running back to get it." I put the envelope in my purse and patted her trembling hand.

Jim still stared, arms folded.

"We parked so far away, it's a wonder you got back for the introductions." I said and looked to Merle for help, but she was still mouth-open stunned by Agnes' scene. I admire people who can only worry about one thing at a time.

"Who was that comin' by your motel room this afternoon? You better answer that 'fore anybody starts anything involvin' you tonight." He leaned dangerously close to her face. She squeezed my hand under the table, like a frightened child.

Then, still holding my hand, she said, "Abby's boyfriend. He lives near here and they don't get to be together much, so we just kinda, you know, got lost for an hour."

There was a long silence. Nelle, Merle and I stared at her with Jim. She looked at me with cow eyes and mouthed, "I'm sorry."

"She sure don't look like the type," Jim said finally and straightened his stance. He touched her shoulder. "I thought he was sissy lookin', and I know what you like, gal."

He pinched and rubbed her upper arm suggestively, then started toward his seat. "No harm meant, ma'am," he said to me, smirked and slowly walked down the aisle.

"You're a good woman to take that, Abby. You saved her." Nelle put her soft, stubby hand on mine.

"You're a good friend," Tamsey whispered without daring to look at me directly.

"No. I'm not a good friend or a good woman. And I resent that redneck ape saying I'm not the type." I laughed. Laughing at myself is one of my few remaining virtues. I wished her accusations were true. Tom Ross had made my heart race.

Merle scurried backstage to get the show started and to adjust her scarf. She walked like a woman with her panties in a wad.

"You know what else I resent?" I said.

Nelle and Tamsey stacked their forms and listened.

"He may be right. I may not be the type that attracts men. Nelle, did you know I have no dates? None. I may not be centerfold material, but I still look better than those bleached blondes who stay booked up, stupid women who wear exercise clothes to the grocery store, please."

I could feel myself on the brink of a full-fledged rant. Nelle cut me off.

"They're just young, Abby. You're gorgeous and you know it. Maybe you're too good looking. A beautiful woman is intimidating to men. Anyway, men our age can still attract much younger women, so they play with twenty-year-olds." She clicked her watermelon pen with finality. "And you can't compete with young."

"I'll try harder," I said. My mind sang very softly and slowly, *Happy Birthday to me.*

A local deejay in a shiny, black tux boomed, "Good evening."

He stood on stage behind an oval microphone on a stand. The crowd hushed and so did the judges.

Doctor J, his WROC listeners called him, but tonight he could have been Master of Ceremonies for Miss Universe. Under the bright circle of lights which rarely left the stage, he was handsome and relaxed.

He began, "Welcome to the 26th Annual Watermelon Festival.

Many of the pageants I've worked with lately have deleted the swim suit competition. One I went to last month substituted an aerobics routine."

Boo's from the crowd.

"Our neighbor, the National Peanut Festival in Dothan, dropped swimsuits entirely. Boy, was I glad to get here, where they know what to look for."

Applause from the audience.

"And we have plenty for you to see tonight."

There was a whistling, cheering crowd response now, which the young MC encouraged by nodding his head knowingly and making a ridiculous curve outline with his hands.

"Tonight, we have three of the finest judges in the South."

The spotlight swung to our table.

"A former Miss Mississippi, now a jewelry designer with her husband's company, Tamsey Pike."

Tamsey stood slowly, waved to the audience on three sides, and turned on a show biz smile she seemed to have borrowed. Her gold dress and wide smile were absolutely dazzling in the glaring light. I saw for the first time how she had done so well in a big pageant a few years and a few pounds ago.

"To her left, a Birmingham, Alabama native who has represented her state in three national pageants, Mrs. Abby Copenhaven."

I stood and faced the crowd, hoping the spotlight didn't annihilate my make-up. Bright light did not do for me what it had just done for Tamsey. I acknowledged the audience on all sides with a gracious smile and took my seat. I refused to wave like a teenager on a parade float.

"Mrs. Copenhaven has two daughters and writes for *Southern Living Magazine*. This year, she has judged sixteen beauty pageants."

I found myself looking through the bright light for Tom Ross.

Nelle stood too soon, just before the announcer said her name.

"Mrs. Nelle Ashford has taught high school English and journalism for twenty years. She lives in Savannah, Georgia with husband Harry Ashford, famous golfer, now the pro at The Tidewater Club. Last year Mrs. Ashford was on the prestigious panel of Miss Georgia for the Miss America Pageant."

Nelle returned to her chair and we three picked up red pens and stacked green folders as if cued.

Columns of dust filled the spotlight as it mercifully shifted back on stage.

"I want to request a moment of silence for a contestant from Fairhope, Alabama who could not be here tonight. Mary Ann Adkins was killed in a school bus accident Wednesday."

Her entry photograph for the pageant was projected onto a white screen set up by the boys directing the spotlight. The beautiful image stayed in place thirty seconds.

The hush was heavy in the auditorium. Most seats were filled with those who knew or loved someone who could have been Mary Ann.

"Our prayers go out to her family." The MC said with bowed head. Yes, he grew up in a Baptist church.

A red velvet curtain opened to a stage too wide for only ten girls. They were randomly placed, wearing miscellaneous swim suits and high heels. Stacked hay bales and watermelons in neat groups of three were the only props. Lazy volunteers, short notice or low budget could not excuse the stage decoration.

The tallest girl on stage introduced herself with a dancer's turn. "I am Sylvia Zorn from LaGrange, Georgia."

"I thought she was going to say Bangladesh," I said through my teeth.

Sylvia's hipbones threatened to puncture her white, Lycra suit. We viewed the hay and watermelons in the background through her frail legs. Her face was starkly beautiful in its gauntness, but should have been seen through a camera lens only.

"She looked a lot better dressed," Tamsey said, cocking her mouth, Popeye style, to one side.

Speaking discreetly is a Southern lady's trait, a talent not far removed from being able to point with a shift of the eyes. If this skill is a gene, Tamsey missed it.

Next, Tonya Ray saluted center stage and clicked her high heels, marched straight toward the audience, then made an about-face to show the low cut back of her navy swim suit. Did she wink over her shoulder?

Daphne Lee Stone moved gracefully on stage and paused for the admiring applause she seemed to expect. At five feet-seven inches, she was tall enough to look elegant and short enough to be well rounded without any real bulk. A jade green swimsuit brought out a hint of gold in her flawless skin. Nelle and I glanced sidelong at Tamsey, who joined us in realizing Daphne was the crowd favorite.

"By the way, what in the hell was going on when I came in?" Tamsey asked during the applause.

"Be innocent of the knowledge, dearest chuck," I answered, eyes focused on the folder in front of me.

"What is wrong with you?" Tamsey was not into Shakespeare.

"Remember, I'm your cover story, your friend," I jabbed. "How quickly they forget."

"I'll make this up to you," Tamsey whispered, afraid I might have second thoughts and damage her with Tom or Jim.

"I had an ex-husband who used to say that, but he never did." I said and put my pen point on the next score sheet.

Then the whinner was stage front, standing too close to the antiquated mic. "Lynn Odom." She began to douse the crowd with the same nasal voice that had made us cringe during the long, only child's interview.

Luwanna Love approached the front apron of the low stage.

Tamsey hiked up one side of her large mouth to comment on her bovine gait.

Under the glaring spotlight, her cheap, red swim suit became pinkish where it stretched over her relaxed stomach.

"All that meat and no potatoes," Tamsey quipped through an ugly side opening she made with her lips.

Nelle responded to the poorly whispered comment, eyes front. "I suppose you like the anorexic girl better."

"I suppose you want a queen who really looks like a watermelon," Tamsey snapped.

"Girls, girls. There's something between Twiggy and a Rubens painting," I said. My analogy was wasted on Tamsey. Her blank expression showed no recognition of model or artist.

Only as Luwanna finished her turn and lumbered off the stage to change, did I spy the hot pink, plastic shoes.

Then little Jeannie Rose marched forward and expertly lowered the oval mic. Only four-inch heels and an inverted design at the top of each leg kept her from looking like a lovable baby-doll in a chic royal blue swim suit. Her stance was a flattering left heel to right arch, with no danger of any light peeking through well-muscled legs.

Had the honorable Jamie been grooming Jeannie, she would not have worn a ponytail which swayed in rhythm to her athletic gait. He would have that thick mane piled high, adding sophistication and height.

I knew Merle Holt's panties must be wadded into a knot by now. The predictable applause changed to wolf whistles and loud clapping when Faye Hightower prissed forward in a pink and black leopard print tank suit. She looked like a glamourous pin-up in a slick magazine. The hot spotlight did for her what it had done for Tamsey a few minutes earlier. Her hair caught the light in soft, wild curls, making it hard to focus on that beautiful face. The same light that showed my age so cruelly, made her glow.

Then, she spoke. Too bad. Nelle touched my arm to keep me from putting my head down on the table. How frustrating to have all that beauty cursed by that tongue.

Faye ran her hand through her hair and shifted sexily.

"She makes my head hurt," I said, not looking up from my blank score sheet.

"She makes my heart hurt," Nelle sighed "So, so beautiful, but. . ."

"But there's just no demand, as they say," Tamsey interrupted, turning her form over with ridiculously long nails.

Nelle sighed again. I caught her mood like a yawn. I'm more easily influenced than anyone I know. In the middle of a crowd, with lives to shatter, and a handsome man to figure out, I managed to catch Nelle's melancholy.

Where does all this get them, anyway?" I asked, safely facing the stage apron.

"Same place it got you and me," Tamsey answered with a yawn, as though I were talking to her. Surely, she and I were not in the same category or the same place in our lives. Surely, she could see that.

I looked at Tamsey for a long time after Candace Young was in place, had said her name and had begun graceful turns in a black swim suit.

Tamsey's eyes and encouraging smile were fixed on the honey blonde.

Up to its old tricks, my brain rushed on without me. For every Bess Myerson, Phyllis George, Diane Sawyer and Mary Ann Mobley, there are ten thousand Tamsey's and Abby's. Queens for a day, then back to the hum drum, grocery store, real life. Jump off that stage and wrap Christmas presents behind a little department store counter or put your grandmother and mother's recipes in *The Junior League Cookbook.*

The hard truth of the arena we were in struck me. I had not arrived. The world had been exposed to me at my dewy prime and had not been impressed, particularly. No doors opened.

The audience applauded, Candace made a curtsy, then a royal wave. She looked as perfect as a mannequin in her swim suit. Not a ripple, just sleek fabric, molded from shoulder to hip.

I really was afraid of anyone that perfect. My brain began the theme song from *The Twilight Zone.*

The smiling MC stopped my song. "Our last contestant, Miss Gloria Byrd."

I was tired at his pretense of being out of breath." Wow, wow." he repeated for the beauties in swim suits.

Gloria, like a white bunny, hopped from her hay bale and hurried to center stage, surprised when her name was called. The spotlight washed away any delicate color that had resided on her pale face. Her hair and eyebrows looked like aspirin bottle cotton. She wore a metallic silver swim suit. In a soft blue spotlight, she might have looked almost angelic.

"How fair she is," Nelle whispered, never turning her head toward me.

How like Nelle, I thought and removed her bitchette title.

Gloria Byrd giggled directly into the microphone, producing painful audio squeal. First, she covered her mouth, then, her ears. Even the hair on her arms glowed in the spot light when she tried to adjust the height of the microphone.

Tamsey began tapping her pen on a folder. She had made her decision and wanted Bunny Cottontail to exit, stage left, so we could get on with it. She was ready to announce the winner and we hadn't gone through the motions of evening gown competition.

There was little applause when Gloria Byrd ran off the stage to change into her gown. Many in the audience were still cupping hands on ears.

The young MC returned. Too much touch up hair spray created a wiggy look under the lights. I couldn't turn off my judging switch and he was the only thing left on stage to judge.

"Boy, oh boy. I would hate to be one of our judges, tonight." The MC suddenly sounded like a recycled DJ.

"I'll bet he would," I said. "If he had to go back to Mississippi with a furious husband."

"Oh, he's OK, now," Tamsey said softly. Softly for her, that is.

"Sure, as long as he thinks Tom Ross is my boyfriend." I looked at the reshuffled score sheets. Number one on top. "Where is my boyfriend, anyway? And which one of these girls is his daughter?"

Tamsey opened and closed her mouth twice. "He didn't hit on you, did he?"

"I wish," I said coolly. I liked taunting Tamsey with what I might know.

"While our beauties are getting ready for the evening gown portion of the pageant, I want to present the new Little Miss Watermelon Festival Princess, Miss Lakeshia Yvonne Johnson."

"My Lord, what a name," Tamsey said while we all clapped.

"I wonder if she can spell it yet," I added.

A tiny girl, about the size my children were at three, walked toward the MC. Her long, blonde curls and wide smile never moved. A red, ruffled dress stood straight out from her waist, so that the MC had to kneel two feet away to hold the mic for her.

She turned her head slowly left and right, never once covering tiny, perfect baby teeth. I was secretly sure her teeth had been glued back in for the pageant. Maybe somebody could do the same for her mother.

Merle pranced to our table under the guise of offering extra pens.

We knew she wanted everyone to see she was still in charge, and perhaps to get a gander at the scores.

"Someone's already grooming that little girl. Can you believe it?" Nelle said.

Merle beamed and flipped her scarf over one shoulder. "You can't start too early in this business." She wheeled dramatically and disappeared into the dark edges of the auditorium.

The baby on stage spoke with a ten- year- old voice. "I'm so happy to represent you as Little Miss Watermelon. I promise to make you proud of me." Only a quick glance at her tattooed, stringy-haired mother in the wings broke her composure. The mother was tapping the underside of her own chin, mouthing "Head up. Head up."

The thin MC stood up. "Now our reigning Festival Queen, Miss Becky Alford, is going to sing for us, Becky."

A fine boned girl with thick, long hair the color of good rye whiskey took the hand mic offered and looped the cord with her free hand like a night club singer. In the brilliant light, her hair could have been labeled red or brown, but her skin had the translucent quality that only red-heads have.

A piano, a drum and an electric guitar, hidden somewhere between the audience and the left side of the stage, played a few measures of *Raindrops Keep Falling on My Head*.

"This should be good," I said to Nelle, who also anticipated the worst. We took a deep breath together and leaned back, ready to look pleasant, regardless of the sound.

"Pretty good," Nelle mouthed.

Then, like a warm glow, her mellow alto voice filled the vaulted spaces of the huge building. Becky's crooning quality was so captivating, a fat mama, intent on running backstage, stopped at the stage side door.

We were all caught by the powerful singing.

Becky held her face toward an imaginary third balcony and threw half-notes like kisses. She walked slowly, first to the left, then to the right of the stage, her vibrant melody flowing effortlessly.

"I don't think she needs that microphone," Nelle said, not taking her eyes from the girl who grew more beautiful as she sang.

Even this audience, here for the sake of their own favorites, clapped, stood, sat down, clapped louder, then stood again. No one knew or dared to call out "Encore" or "Bravo." It didn't matter. Becky Alford might not have known how to respond.

"Can you believe her? For once, Old Merle knew what she was talking about." Tamsey said, applauding enthusiastically. "Give her a number and we'll solve all our problems."

"It's a shame there's no talent in this pageant," Nelle said,

"Oh, I don't know. We could count comedy," I said.

"Stop that," Nelle laughed.

"She was wonderful, really professional," I said.

"I'd be afraid of anybody that perfect." Tamsey threw in her sarcastic little ace and I folded.

Nelle had been at this game longer. "Of course, talent is a real thing, not like memorized answers."

"Forget it," Tamsey snapped. It was not with Nelle she wanted to spar, but me. Her gratitude had not replaced her resentment at being found out.

My mind escaped the mundane reality of the auditorium. How simple life would be if we balanced our emotions, like the amount of water displaced by a submerged object in a lab. No, we choose to keep all the worry, not just the old problem, but the new pain that replaced it. If emotions reacted like the laws of physics, there would be no grand pile up of stress.

My eyes caught the red curtain closing and I stopped my wandering brain in its tracks. I looked about subtly for Tom Ross and saw Tamsey doing the same.

When the velvet curtain opened again, a single, white Dorian column, flanked by two enormous ferns adorned the stage. I noted one was a Boston and the other a petticoat type, placed by a volunteer decorating committee, no doubt.

With a drum roll, the MC boomed out the contestants' names in a rapid rhythm that set my mind to reciting "On Dancer, on Prancer, on Donner and Blitzen."

More rapid than eagles the girls swirled around the column to parade in a full circle.

There she stood. "Look." I nudged Nelle and pointed with my eyes.

Agnes was next to the MC, cradling the individual red roses, wrapped in ribbons and baby's breath. She handed them to him stupidly, one at a time, to present to each girl, as she reached her mark taped on stage. Agnes never looked at the MC, the contestants or the audience, only the roses.

Without warning, Agnes raised her puffy eyes and glared at me.

"Please," The MC whispered, while he tugged at the rose she held tightly. "Let go."

Now the timing was off and a gap developed in the line of multi-colored gowns. Lynn Odom bumped into Luwanna Love, who turned on her, remembered she wasn't at the Piggly Wiggly and continued the parade.

Nelle touched my knee with hers under the folding table and pointed her pen toward the left. A small man, hand on hip, stood in the audience.

Daphne Stone made a double turn on stage, white sequined gown floating in the light. The audience applauded.

"Yes," Jamie mouthed as he returned to his seat by his client. He caught us looking and winked at our table. Confidence in his girl was what he sold and he was good at it.

"Ladies, please give the judges another view." They all faced the rear of the stage, all turned left in unison. The better coached girls looked artfully over one shoulder.

"Turn once again, please." When the MC hit "please," they all pivoted to face us. Nelle put her pen down. I followed her signal.

"Nothin' left but the shoutin'," Tamsey said and closed her folder, nodded to the MC and pushed her chair back.

"There won't be any shouting. Just one, two, three. We know the three, let's put them in order and go home," I said.

"Thank you, girls," Dr. J, now a refined MC, said. They filed off stage, heads right, as rehearsed, giving everyone concerned a last look.

We were not concerned and hurried to a small room just off the stage stairs. Merle was already there. She positioned a gray metal chair at the end of the only table in the room before we could close the door against the auditorium noise.

"I'll help you tally," she said.

The tap dancing routine on stage, planned to fill the lull, also filled the small, attic shaped room under the stage with a series of rhythmical shuffle hop steps. I knew the steps from the sounds.

I had once loved tap dancing, but when a sorority sister pointed out how un-elegant, even vulgar some of the steps were, I shifted to modern jazz. I suppose jazz dancing was more acceptable for a 5'10" girl. I guess neither would be very acceptable now.

Before Nelle could muster a protest over the echoing taps and pushy director, Agnes pushed in, slamming the door behind her.

"You Yankee sluts, you did this." She brandished a rolled program like a summons to hell. "As God is my witness, you'll live to pay for this."

No one moved. Only the shuffle, hop, step above us counted the silent seconds. I wanted to whisper to Nelle that Agnes could play Scarlet O'Hara, but thought better of it.

"Agnes! What's come over you? Using that kind of language to these ladies, shame." Merle said. "What would make you call them Yankees?"

I noted no defense was made for being sluts.

"What is she talking about?" Tamsey said and turned her back on the awkward girl. "Git her out of here. She's holding up the show."

"Come along, Agnes. Whatever has made you so angry can be explained, I'm sure." Merle put her arm around Agnes' stooped shoulders.

"Read it and weep." Agnes sounded like an ancient prophetess when she slapped the crumpled program on the table.

"A bad case of too many old movies," I said, safe in the knowledge that Agnes was only guessing the source of her trauma.

"I don't see anything to get upset about. You're wasting our time. So, what if your name's misspelled or something," Tamsey said, reading the program.

Chapter Seventeen

THE TALLY

"Y ou go to Hell!" Agnes screamed. And count your own points up, if you can." She shook off Merle's arm and banged the door behind her, lifting loose papers all over the desk and floor.

Gathering and sorting them, I spied Tamsey's tally sheet.

She covered it with forms and tried to catch my eye to judge how much I had seen. Well, I've watched a few old movies, too. Shirley Temple would have been hard pressed to look more innocent.

"I don't think you should be in here, Merle," Nelle said. "We'll just be five minutes."

"But you need someone to add up and someone to put the final scores in this envelope for the MC."

"My God. You only have ten contestants. I can add. Tamsey can lick the envelope, I think," I said.

Merle Holt was determined. She opened the door quietly, then without warning yelled, "Judge Wilson."

"What are you doing?" Nelle stood up as Hiram Wilson, probate judge and lifetime Watermelon Festival board member, lumbered in.

Judge Wilson, stomach preceding him like a separate entity, puffed into the small space, giving me instant claustrophobia.

"These ladies will each give you their number one, two and three choices. You will tally them and give the name of the queen and two runners-up to Dr. J, up there on the stage. Here. Use this envelope."

Merle was in charge again and gloried in it. "Three points for each number one vote, two points for each second-place vote, and one point

102

for a third- place vote. Got it?" She now stood between the old, pink-faced judge and our table, no easy maneuver.

"Glad to serve the festival in any capacity, dear lady," he said and stepped aside to allow Merle to leave.

He bowed slightly toward us. "Yo servant."

We had been reared in the South and recognized the power of a big, gentlemanly politician when it literally surrounded us.

Tamsey folded and submitted her form on the spot.

With my eyes, I alerted Nelle that Tamsey had stacked her deck for her girl, Candace. Nelle smiled sweetly, and we wrote simultaneously.

The gray suited hulk sat on the metal chair Merle had vacated. I had new respect for folding chairs. His eye was quicker than his sluggish body. In ten seconds he digested all scores into winner and runners-up, and jotted the numbers on a thick, green card, which he sealed in the red envelope.

"Well?" I asked, waiting for his revelation.

"Come on out in the audience, ladies, and join the fun." He chuckled and left the room.

"He and Merle are in cahoots. I know it." Tamsey stood up and bumped her head on the slanted stair wall. "Damn it to hell."

"Tamsey, are you alright?" Nelle was concerned, motherly for a moment.

I had lost count of the mother in Nelle surfacing, as well as the other side games my mind had set out to play.

Tamsey nodded and lifted her hair with her long nails. "By the way, I want to thank ya'll for coverin' for me with Jim. I was scared. He's a good man, but he gets real rough if you cross him."

"You're brave to cross him, then. I hope Tom Ross was worth it."

"Oh, God, yes." Tamsey closed her eyes. "Yes, yes, yes."

I couldn't feel sorry for her, now. Maybe she deserved to be battered. What's wrong with me? Nobody deserves that, not even Miss Hot to Trot.

"You don't know how brave. Last year I thought I had a broken arm, and I wasn't seein' anybody then." Tamsey touched her left elbow and closed her eyes for a slow blink. "Yeah, I was real scared. You know how it is with men." She stood up slowly this time.

No, I didn't know. I understood dread, avoiding confrontation, but never fear, not pick your own switch in the back-yard fear, not child fear of inescapable punishment, not beaten until you beg fear.

"Can we hear from down here?" I asked.

"Let's go out and see the winner," Tamsey said.

We knew she wanted to look for Tom Ross. Nelle and I exchanged quick stink-eye squints. I knew Tamsey had put Candace as number one and completely omitted Anna, substituting Daphne Stone in second and Nelle's little Jeannie in third. If I knew Nelle, she wouldn't dare leave my girl off entirely. I felt sure she placed her favorite as the winner, but I could only guess if she included Candace. Perhaps my last-minute eye contact had backed Nelle away from Candace. Maybe she considered Merle's bad reputation warning.

"It's never a good idea to go back into the arena, you know. It can become the Christians and the lions, once the queen is crowned," Nelle said.

"The trouble is nobody can decide who the Christians are," I added.

"I don't care. I've got to see this." Tamsey led the way.

"I wonder if this is her first-time judging." Nelle whispered behind me as we followed.

Merle appeared in the hall suddenly. "Hurry up."

"One question," I said as we followed her into the auditorium. "Which one is Tom Ross' daughter?"

Merle stopped so abruptly that I ran into her. She wheeled to face me. "Daughter! Daughter?" She threw her head back and laughed an old lady stage cackle. "You are kidding me, right? Please, tell me you are joking." She shook her head.

We moved through the crowd to our long table near the stage's apron and took our seats.

"Second runner-up, Anna Livingston," The MC shouted.

My lovely librarian moved forward in a simple, white gown. She would have made a refined, classy queen. She looked thrilled to have placed.

I clapped numbly, letting my mind run ahead in a vague equation, close to simple deduction.

Tamsey did not move.

"First runner-up and alternate queen if circumstances prevent the winner from fulfilling her duties. . ."

"Get on with it, Goober," Tamsey whispered through her teeth.

"Number seven, Jeannie Rose."

Nelle and I looked at each other, minus smirks.

"I can't believe we let this happen," Nelle mumbled.

On stage, Jeannie was engulfed by taller girls, hugging and kissing her. Everyone was surprised, but not unhappy. Besides, there was still the queen to be announced.

Tamsey clasped her hands, elbows resting on the table. She craned her head looking for Jim, but he had left during the tap dancing. She pulled her hands apart, at the ready to burst into applause for herself and Tom's daughter. She wisely refused to meet our stares.

Becky Alford moved to the MC's side, crown and banner poised.

Flanking the MC's right was poor Agnes. She looked like a wet, long haired dog next to the girls on stage. She held a tall trophy to her chest, both arms folded all the way around it. At a less than subtle signal from Merle, she held the gold colored loving cup by its ornate vine handles.

Laughter broke out behind us. Judge Hiram Wilson stood in front of both the MC and Becky. At a gentle tug from the MC, he pushed in between them.

He held a huge oval watermelon known as a rattlesnake, due to its stripes. Trying to hand off the specimen watermelon to Becky Alford, the judge dropped it. The beautiful singer had to choose between the crown and the heavy watermelon. Dresses and shoes in a six-foot radius were splashed with pink juice.

"And the winner and new Watermelon Festival Queen is number four, Daphne Lee Stone." The MC shouted over the crowd, as though she had been his favorite, all along.

Chapter Eighteen

SECOND CHOICE

The stage was Bedlam with watermelon juice, tears and embraces, but Candace Young and Tamsey Pike were frozen. I looked just beyond Tamsey and saw Jamie and his blonde companion. They were jumping and shouting, congratulating each other, as though Daphne was not a part of their success.

Ah, the mother, I thought. She has no idea how convoluted all this is. She is giving thanks to us and to Jamie.

Candace looked blankly into the audience. She was isolated from the bumping embraces and Vaseline coated lipstick smears of the girls on stage. Her eyes sought out her champion.

Now Tamsey turned to me. "I don't understand. I feel sick. Look at her up there. Candace should be the winner and she knows it. We know it. He knows it."

Tom Ross approached the stage and lifted Candace down to floor level and held her.

We heard Jim before we saw him. I smelled his bourbon breath when he shouted, "Why'd you come with somebody else's boyfriend? Maybe you're two-timin' your judge friend and your husband, you ungrateful bitch."

"She may be only a bitchette," I said, knowing I could never explain the levels and subtle differences of bitchlets, bitchettes and bitches. Most people don't understand the concept and no men do. I don't know why I said it.

He grabbed Tamsey by the back of her neck and pulled her face close to his. She did not resist.

"Do I need to call security?" Nelle said and touched my arm in a weak attempt to remove me from the fray.

"You can call security after I beat his eyes together," I said. I had seen security. It was Barney Fife's daddy in a mismatched uniform and tennis shoes.

Jim Pike leaned over me. "Are you two covering up for each other?" he slurred while I focused on the bar-b-que sauce on his thin mustache.

Nelle stood up and pushed her chair back with her short legs "She is fucking crazy and can kill you with a credit card, man. Back off."

Nelle said fuck. The world as I know it is coming to an end. I might as well crawl under this table now.

Big Diamond Jim let Tamsey go, straightened up and walked to the back of the auditorium.

"Holy crap on a cracker," Tamsey whispered.

She took a few steps toward Tom. "I feel so bad for them. It breaks my heart." Tamsey said.

Just then we saw Tom's hand pat Candace's butt. She kissed him too long.

"Son of a bitch. Daughter, my ass," Tamsey said and tried to step around Nelle to get to Tom.

"We have to go. You've got Jim and this crowd to worry about right now. I don't like it," Nelle said.

The crowd surged forward. A few people studied us, but most had their gaze on the stage. I saw Luwanna Love's mother moving toward us. She filled the center aisle, pushing against the flow.

"Let's get to our cars, while the gettin's good," I said and picked up my purse. Merle appeared out of nowhere and blocked my path.

"Don't worry. You did right. I told you about that girl." She looked toward Candace who was still draped over Tom.

"Sorry, babe, you can't win them all," Tom said and pushed her toward an exit. They pressed through the crowd by us, so close we could hear Tom's bass whispers soothing her tears.

All movement stopped after Hiram Wilson dropped the watermelon. Local news people flashed away, feeling lucky to find anything news worthy here.

Nelle touched my elbow to let me know she was right behind me.

We needed Tamsey to run interference, but she was not cooperating. She could not take her glare off Tom and Candace.

From the looks on stage, none of the girls considered what transpired luck. In a pageant, girls hope to be lucky. They pray and cross fingers. But when they win, they believe it was all them.

"Another night, another judge, another winner." I had said it so often, it was almost Biblical.

Tamsey joined our little train headed toward an exit. "Damn poor planning, if you ask me." She looked around for another exit and Merle in the crowd.

My brain raced, as my feet stopped. I felt anger at the blatant disregard for common decency and protocol. "How dare them," I lowered my voice for Nelle's ears only.

"Are you angry that Tamsey had a fling right in front of us, or that Candace almost won because of a dishonest judge?" Nelle said to my back.

"All that," I answered over my shoulder. "She's using us. Does she think we're stupid?"

"Magna cum dumb ass," Nelle replied.

A synapse suddenly connected Texas and use good judgement from the note still in my purse. The west exit door was locked. The whole audience pushed for the same east exit. Anyone could be ambushed leaving through the lone door, maybe a judge who didn't pick the only Texas girl in the pageant.

Mind, how you do go on. I thought.

Merle was on the stage, where she had pushed between Daphne and her Mother to start preening the poor girl for Houston.

A hard spot formed in my stomach. Daphne Lee Stone had been Merle's choice all along. She had tried to sway us from the strongest challenger, Candace, then had called old Judge Wilson as insurance, at the last minute, to tally and submit a winner.

I hoped Tamsey couldn't fit the puzzle together, at least not until she got home. Hindsight is painful and the sooner a mistake, like being out-maneuvered by the likes of Merle Holt is realized, the worse the pain.

I disliked Merle and all her clones across the South, but we were to blame, too. Our power plays made it possible for her to sweep in with Daphne. Nelle had warned us.

I wondered how common it was for the winner not to be the top choice of any of the judges.

We were immobile again. The poorly dressed crowd pressed on all sides. "This is worse than football traffic," I said.

"Let's hope it's not worse than Mobile," Nelle said. "Stay right with us, Tamsey."

Tamsey caught the note of danger in Nelle's voice and surged us forward a few feet as a unit of three.

"What happened in Mobile?" Tamsey shouted, closing ranks to avoid a buxom woman carrying a fat baby.

Á furious father jumped Nelle and me in the parking lot after a pageant. Thank God, a State Trooper's daughter was in the contest and he parked near us."

I shortened the story, since I had to shout.

"Was she like my girl tonight?" Even Tamsey had enough sense not to shout Candace's name.

The outcomes of the pageants had nothing in common. The Mobile affair was so much grander, better orchestrated, that I couldn't begin to explain.

Nelle filled in when I hesitated. A beautiful Black girl was a runner-up. That's what pushed him over the edge, more than his daughter not placing. There were fifty-two girls in the pageant, but the Black one placing over his daughter was too much for him. He was pouring gasoline on Abby's new car when we walked up on him."

"Wonder why there wasn't a single Black girl in this pageant." Tamsey said.

"What Black girl in her right mind," I could not shout over the increasing crowd noise.

Everyone was anxious to get out of the building. Finally, the security guard figured out how to unchain the other exit and we made headway. Now a couple of parents way-laid us.

"What can I do to score higher next year?" An anorexic looking girl asked. She was in my space, only inches from my face.

I couldn't think which contestant she was. I was getting

claustrophobic. Before I could form a polite reply, a brassy mother on my left pushed her red-eyed daughter in front of Nelle and me.

"Critique her right quick, please ma'am. We've got two more contests comin' up before Christmas."

Nelle looked at me for help. It was the only child whinner.

I wanted to say, "You are a skinny, country, tacky, nasal, ridiculous brat. Stay home." Instead I listened and smiled approval while Nelle suggested she work on her walk.

I turned back toward the exit and there was the tall Zorn girl with her taller, gaunt Father. "Give her some advice." He said and pushed her forward.

"Maybe you could gain a little weight before the next swimsuit competition," I said, softly.

"You're crazy!" she shouted in my face. "What did you expect from a bunch of fat, old women?" She turned her anger toward her father.

"We coulda used that money for school, you know," her father said as they snatched themselves away from us.

"So much for truth, I said to Nelle.

"Avoid truth like the plague when a parent asks you to critique a child," Nelle advised.

Stopped again. Now the white bunny girl had Tamsey. Nelle took over, we had to get out.

"We have a plane to catch, dear, sorry." Nelle retrieved Tamsey and we walked faster, but not fast enough.

"Just tell me how I can do better in the Maid of Cotton Pageant in January."

Giggling Gloria wasn't laughing when she caught up with us. She was supported by her two albino-like parents, a frightening trio.

I wanted to ask if she believed in reincarnation. Instead my hypocritical lips said, "Now, Maid of Cotton, that might be your cup of tea, your kind of pageant."

At last we stepped outside into the hot, moist Summer air of the gravel parking lot. After searching the perimeter with nervous eyes, I looked at Nelle and Tamsey to bask in their laughter about the Maid of Cotton quip, nothing. It gets old laughing at your own humor.

The security guard in a faded blue shirt, once part of a uniform, approached us. "I was 'spose to escort ya'll to your cars, but thought I'd mist ya in the crowd." He spat tobacco neatly. "Miss Merle said you'd prolly be leavin' early."

Nelle and I pointed to the far edge of the lot. Tamsey trailed us, not sure where she had left her car.

A tall young man in a white knit shirt ran toward us with an urgent message. "Road Whores!" he screamed as he swerved past us. "Hope you got plenty of money for leaving out the prettiest girl in the whole damn pageant." He had tears in his eyes.

Tamsey stared after him. "A boyfriend."

The security guard took a few mock running steps after the angry young man, then caught up with us. "'scuse him, ladies. He's just hot because Faye Hightower didn't win. That's his girl. He's the one takin' all the pictures."

Our escort looked back at the running figure disappear around the corner of the building. "No real harm in him."

"Right here." Nelle patted the back window of her car.

"And them?" The old man pointed.

"Abby and I are together. Tamsey, where are you parked?" Nelle asked.

"I'm in the next row, I think." She looked around once more for Jim, or maybe Tom Ross, who knows. A man like Tom can make a woman stupid.

"OK. Have a safe trip." Our armed escort said, already walking back toward the auditorium. He waved once in the air, not turning around.

"Some send-off," I said and held my purse a little tighter.

There was a long silence as we stood behind Nelle's big Buick.

"When shall we three meet again?" Nelle said in a shockingly good Scottish accent. She broke the strained dilemma of parting and knowing too much about each other's weaknesses.

"In thunder, lightning or in rain?" I replied, stirring an imaginary cauldron.

We both looked to Tamsey to complete our witchy quotation.

"Well, ya'll be careful and thanks for everything. Oh, I want you to know, no hard feelings. We all lost, in a way."

"Hey, girl." It was Jim one row behind us, leaning on Tamsey's gold Cadillac with TAMSEY on the license plate.

"Of course, that's her car," I said.

"I've been waitin' on you. Let's get a late bite somewhere," he spoke softly.

"I don't know, Jim." She was already walking toward him.

"Come on, baby, you can drive. I'll follow you home in the morning." He looked back at us. "Sorry, ladies."

"Tamsey, you OK?" Nelle called out.

"Don't make me come down there," I called loudly.

"No ma'am. We're OK," Jim answered in a drunk, but repentant voice. He got in the passenger side.

"She would have fit right in with some of tonight's girls," Nelle said, digging in her purse for keys.

"Maybe I would have, too, thirty years ago," I said.

The pink glow in the parking lot lightened gravity's power on our faces. I forgot between pageants how short Nelle was. "What's your next pageant?"

"Possum Queen," she answered.

We laughed. "Really," I said.

"Miss Lake Lanier," Nelle said. "Then, Miss Columbus. Only one week between them."

I walked around to the passenger side of her car. "Oh no, will you look at this!"

Nelle ran to my rescue, then stopped abruptly at my side. "No need to smell to see if it's gasoline." She said and fished a roll of paper towels from the depths of her purse. In one delft sweep, she removed the round pile of cow manure balanced above my door.

A resounding little plop and escape of odor showed it was fresh.

"I never thought I'd be relieved to find cow plop on my door."

"Cow plop," Nelle repeated. "You have such a way with words."

We hugged each other and laughed at the pageant, the whole system, ourselves.

"She must have been everybody's second choice," I said.

"I'm not a math major, but I think two and two and two is still six. Three second placements won over Anna with a first, a third and a zero from Tamsey. Then, my first- place vote for Jeannie with a third- place vote from you and Tamsey makes a total of five points to be runner-up."

My mind went into crazy mode. It goes there too often, now. Maybe I had won all thirteen pageants as everybody's second choice. Maybe I wasn't queen material, so I kept winning. Was that how it was?

I had been a cocky winner at times. Once spinning around on the ball of one foot like a dancer. Another time I bowed before an incredibly short queen to receive my crown. I made it look like a curtsy.

The old MC started the audience clapping, saying, "That's how it's done, son."

Little did I know.

I got into the passenger side, closed the heavy door and saw Tom Ross at my window. He leaned in. "Son of a bitch," I whispered.

"Sorry about the daughter thing." He tried to open the door. I locked it.

"She hangs out at my house all the time and I guess I tried to help her in the wrong way. Everything else I said was true. Her mother died last year. My ex-wife died ten years ago, a long time after we divorced."

I raised the window. I wished the cow plop was there to fall on his head.

"I want to see you again. I'm taking Candace home, her home."

"What about Tamsey?" I was angry and embarrassed, but still drawn to him.

"Come on. She's married. I didn't know it. She set up our meeting. It was nothing to me. OK, that was mistake, too."

"Oh, Please," Nelle said sarcastically. She craned her short neck to check on Tamsey and Jim's progress.

Despite the parking lot's hazy glow, I saw Tamsey looking at Tom Ross talking to me. How painful for her ego. If I had known the extreme vamp she put on him in their hurried hour, I would not have asked about her. In the interest of time, she had straddled him and finally bitten him as he climaxed. How foolish to feel a little triumphant over her when I had only talked to him. How foolish to still be here.

I pushed his proffered card back to him and made the mistake of touching him. There was electricity. I think we both made and felt it. He sucked his breath in.

"What did you tell Candace? Isn't she waiting in your car for you?" Why was I still talking to him?

Tom ducked his head. "OK, you got me. She thinks I'm giving you judges a piece of my mind."

"You jerk." I wanted to run over him, twice.

"Drive, Nelle."

Tamsey and Jim watched Tom Ross walk toward his car on their row. Jim smiled at him and gave him a thumbs-up gesture.

Tamsey glared at me through thirty feet of parking lot and headlights.

When we pulled out of our space, Nelle blew her breath out noisily. "Give me that card." She held out her hand. "I cannot believe your bad judgement. What is wrong with you? Does he have to wear a sign? I am a heart breaker. Come get some!"

"I guess I'm better at judging women than men. Always have been."

I gave her the card. She was always right.

Part II

NEGOTIATIONS

"Don't start none, won't be none." The UPS lady said, checking Robert Wheaton's signature on her form. "Your editor is on a tear this morning, girl." She rushed by me in brown shorts made for a man.

The magazine office's receptionist, Ida Cummings, nodded in agreement.

Ida was thirty-five, smiling and efficient, while appearing to be disinterested in office business. She knew everybody and their business. She had crazy hair, was athletic and smart, with a circle of brainy girlfriends who camped and hiked with her.

Great. I wanted to explain to my editor why I could not go to Houston. The late August air was Africa hot and I was worn out. How could judging the National Agriculture Pageant help our magazine?

"Come in, Abby. Ida will bring you a cup of coffee."

Ida rolled her eyes which showed late-night margarita bags.

"No. thank you, too hot."

"You plan to fly or drive to Houston?" Robert Wheaton stacked papers on his huge desk.

"Neither, sir." I had to show respect to escape a tirade, his MO when refused anything. He usually started with trying to make me feel like an ungrateful child.

"That Mississippi woman is having surgery or something and the committee called me to get you. The US Agriculture Commissioner remembers you, requested you. Do you know how much advertising he throws our way?"

"Plenty of people can replace an old beauty queen."

"They want you." He took off his glasses and stared me down.

"You volunteered me," I said without looking away.

"This time, you're wrong." He moved his glasses on his desk.

"You know what PR is to a publisher? Not Pain in the Rear, my dear." He smiled at his rhyme.

"I just came back from the Chesapeake Bay shoot. Give me a break."

"Break my heart," he said.

Can a man be a bitch? I remained silent. Maybe he would take pity on me if I looked down.

"David Dodd will be there. I know you listen to his talk show. And somebody who used to play for the Houston Oilers. Can't remember his name, but he's famous. You follow football?"

He stood to dismiss me. I did not move. He had to do better than that. Passive-aggressive negotiations are my specialty.

"You may have to get a new evening gown for the televised night," he offered. "I understand Houston has better shopping than Birmingham."

Nobody has better shopping than Birmingham, Alabama. But like Brer Rabbit, I just laid low.

Testosterone is a dangerous thing, even in a soft-handed, silk suited editor. He had to win. I waited.

"OK. Go a day early and take in a spa. It'll make you feel rested." He was desperate. He must have promised a beauty pageant judge to someone way up the totem pole.

"You owe me." I left his office with a defeated expression.

When the door closed, Ida got up and bumped my hip with hers. What an eaves dropper she was!

"Neiman Marcus and a spa day. You are the best," she said.

"Yes, I am."

Chapter Nineteen

THE DRIVER

Tom Ross was waiting for me at the Houston Airport.

"Are you meeting someone?" I said in greeting.

"You. I'm waiting to take you to dinner."

He looked younger than I remembered. God, I thrilled again to that deep voice.

"Really? How did you know I was coming? Why are you here? I have to pick up a rental car. I need to get my luggage." I was talking too fast and avoiding his eyes.

"I have your car. I'll take you to your hotel and dinner. Patrice Wilson asked me to be your driver." He paused. "You know, the pageant director."

He was smiling like a naughty little boy. "Now, I'll tell you the truth, the Ag commissioner and I go way back. He owes me. Being your driver squares us up."

"What?" All that about PR and commissioner and sick judge was a lie. How far would this man go?

"Let's go get your bags."

"Bag, I travel light." And shop heavy, now that I seem to be valuable currency.

We walked in the heat to short term parking. A black Mercedes sedan opened its trunk for my suitcase and carry-on.

"Is this my car?"

"This week it is, with a good driver."

He opened the passenger door and kissed my forehead before I realized his intent. I ignored the sweet gesture. No thank you, no thank you. Nelle's advice rang in my ears, but so did his voice.

"It's not hard. No thank you is all you need to say. Not because he did this or said that, you don't need a reason." Nelle was always right.

"I have to say no thank you to dinner." My smile was shaky.

"I'll pass that on to the pageant committee. I'm just the driver." He backed out of the small space and patted my knee at the same time. I was in trouble.

The ride to the Four Seasons was quiet. Sixties music added a little comfort to an awkward silence.

My bitch gene surfaced. It will out, despite all consequences. "Have any daughters in this one?"

"I'm sorry about all that. Let it go, please."

Let it go? It's the only thing besides Nelle's voice keeping me from climbing on your lap, I thought.

The staff at the hotel treated me like royalty. Without any waiting or wandering in the huge lobby, I was in a VIP elevator. A beautiful, young Mexican man opened my suite. It was filled with roses and had a bottle of chilled champagne on a small white draped table.

"May I pour a glass for you?" The well-trained man asked.

"Certainly, is there a card? I mean for the flowers." I rummaged in my bag for reading glasses and a tip. The yellow note was there. I couldn't throw it away. It had to be an omen.

"May I read it to you?"

I shook my head yes.

"See you at seven in the main lobby. T."

Two hours to get myself together. Call Nelle? Call Tom to regret? I had no idea how to contact my driver. I have to eat. I paced the large room. Tomorrow is my spa day. Maybe they have a treatment to cleanse him out of my system.

I sang *I'm gonna wash that man right out of my hair and send him on his way.* My singing and my humor are better when I'm alone.

I dressed for dinner too quickly and was antsy about waiting and thinking and not calling Nelle.

I toured the grotto-like spa to fill the time. Manicure, pedicure, facial and massage were scheduled for tomorrow afternoon, a visit to old Neiman in the morning. I wondered what time the store opened.

Friday would be business as usual. Interviews in the morning, show time at seven. The girls had been rehearsing for days. The director always hired an orchestra and that made everything harder.

Last year the choreographer spent his time stamping his feet for the orchestra to stop, shouting over the music, and crying backstage. Maybe he had better dancers in the line-up this year. That thought made me laugh out loud.

"What are you laughing about?" Tom Ross was waiting in the lobby.

"You're early," I said, tugging at the black pant suit-gone-tuxedo-without a shirt, too much cleavage, too late to change.

"Must not be too early, you're here. You look stunning."

OK, he's seen my cleavage. "Thank you." I should be saying no thank you.

"Can you walk in those shoes?" he asked.

I squinted my eyes, level with his, thanks to three- inch heels. "I can run in these shoes."

"I'll just bet you can," he said. "The restaurant is only a block away."

"Fine."

"Fine," he imitated me.

We walked the short block without talking until I fell. I never fall. My heel caught in a pavement crack and I fell like a cartoon character, face first.

"This is my fault. Where are you hurt?"

"My hand." I held up the heel of my hand, scraped and bleeding. "I guess I caught myself."

He pulled me upright. He smelled like sweet limes. "You didn't turn an ankle, did you?" He bent down and felt both ankles. Glad I shaved my legs. For balance, I put both hands on his bent back. How was I comfortable with this?

"They look OK."

"Just OK?" We both laughed softly.

"We're here. Let's get that hand cleaned up," he said.

A large band-aid later, we ate thick, rare rib eyes with roasted asparagus and mushrooms. My second glass of Merlot made me relaxed and talkative.

"Why are you going to all this trouble, Tom Ross?" I liked saying his name.

"I think I need someone like you in my life, you know, an anchor," he said.

"Like a millstone around your neck to keep you at home?" I wanted an argument, a reason to leave mad, call Nelle, tell her how strong I was.

"Stability, respectability, I need a rope to hold on to against the tide of my nature. When I saw you, I knew you were it. Then I screwed it up. I was ashamed of the stupid position I was in."

"Let me get this straight. Am I your beard?"

"My life-line," he reached across the small table and held my good hand. I swear I felt an electric current.

"Please excuse me," I said.

He half stood and I grabbed my evening bag. Was I going to the ladies' room, to the lobby to call Nelle, or to the front door to run back to the hotel? My heart was beating too fast and I felt a pleasant light-headedness.

I leaned against an elegant marble counter in the lobby and called Nelle. "I'm having dinner with Tom Ross. I'm scared."

"You should be. He's a lying bastard who would screw a striped snake if somebody held its head." Nell sounded furious.

"So, you're saying you don't approve?"

"Don't make me come down there," Nelle teased.

"I'm crazy about him and I hardly know him," I whispered.

"You know plenty. Open your eyes. We all watched Doris Day movies, but most of us didn't take notes. Don't be taken in. Go home. Say no thank you."

There was a long phone lull. "I know you're right. You're always right. That's why I called you. It's just so hard to say no." My voice cracked. She could not know I was crying. I am a grown-ass woman.

"Call you tomorrow with the low down on the judges. Wait! Did I tell you Dean Kathleen Ward from Auburn is a judge? No, I couldn't make that up. Those girls better shape up or they'll be on social probation."

"Love you, too." I returned to our table.

"How about dessert? We can share. Crème Brule?" Tom said.

"My favorite, and a cup of coffee." We settled in like an old couple.

"Sorry I was so forward. Don't let me scare you away. I'll try to act normal, if you'll let me stay around you a little."

He sounded sad. My instinct was to comfort him. No thank you.

Back in the oasis of my room, I felt disappointed that I had not kissed him at the elevator. That would have been safe enough, but I needed to talk to Nelle again without anything to confess.

"Hey. It's me again. Am I calling too late?" I asked.

Nelle's voice was soft, but not sleepy. She was worried.

"Did he go home peacefully?" she asked.

"I didn't even kiss him goodnight. I was afraid to. I didn't pack fancy panties."

We laughed. "I didn't have to say no thank you."

"He won't give up, you know," Nelle warned.

I told her about the commissioner's role in setting me up, the flowers, the car.

"Text book," Nelle said. "If you let that dog break your heart, I will kill him and beat your butt."

"Can Catholics do that?" I asked.

"Oh, we do worse than that," Nelle said. "And get forgiveness for it."

"Why am I attracted to bad boys?" I whined like a teenager.

"Have we had this discussion?" Nelle answered.

"You can't allow anyone you don't trust into your circle. You have daughters who put you on a pedestal, for good reason. You cannot afford to damage their security or yours. Nobody said it was easy to be a good woman."

"Nelle, I'm only good on the outside. I want to be bad. Did you know that?" I was on the cusp of a full-blown squalling jag. "Maybe I am bad, but don't look the part."

"Stop it. Everybody wants to do wrong sometimes. It's turning your back on opportunities to sin, refusing to wrong someone, keeping peace that makes you a good woman. We are role models without ever giving our permission."

"Who made those rules? Some Catholic man?" I said to start Nelle on a rant. No, that dog won't hunt. It's me who rants.

"Three more days. No thank you, no, thank you."

"Good night. Call me tomorrow." She hung up and I held the phone like a hand.

The bedside phone rang. Why would he call thirty minutes after our date?

"I wanted to talk to you some more." It was Nelle's voice.

"Think about what you need in a partner. List all the things you want in a man before you go to sleep tonight. We aren't twenty any more. You need someone who has your best interest at heart. You need a giver, not a taker. People don't change much. Find an even-tempered man without much baggage."

"Nelle, Ward Cleaver is dead."

"Call me tomorrow. Don't do anything foolish," she said.

The phone rang again. What a nag Nelle was turning into." What?" I answered loudly.

"They teach you that in charm school?" Tom's deep voice sounded too close to my face on the phone.

"What are you, a stalker?"

"I just wanted to hear your voice before I went to bed."

"Goodnight."

"I could really get used to you."

"Goodnight, Tom Ross."

The background music and laughter did not come from a bedroom, but a bar. I was looking for lies, looking for anything to justify throwing something like Tom Ross away.

Chapter Twenty

THE REHEARSAL

A
fter the luxury of a room service breakfast, I wandered down to the huge convention ballroom. Rehearsals should be in full swing. Interviews were sometimes fast and furious, so I wanted an anonymous head-start.

I sat in the back, as far as possible from the stage.

"May I join you?" a middle aged, sturdy woman in a navy linen suit and a pink blouse sat a seat away from me. "Dean Kathleen Ward, Auburn University." She shook my hand. "Dean of Women," she said.

"Abby Copenhaven, I'm just watching a few minutes of the rehearsal."

"I thought you were a judge, too. This is my first time. I can't wait to meet Linda Levine. I watched her sitcom for years."

I really need to read that packet when I get back to the room. Patrice Wilson had a formula in her pageants. Her five judges always consisted of a celebrity, a sports figure, an educator, a politician and a past beauty queen.

How can the Dean of Women, whose primary job is to rule on social probation hearings and preside over women's convocation ceremonies, judge a national beauty pageant?

The music was loud and made it difficult for the Dean of Women to chat. I made no eye contact. I wanted to watch the contestants on stage.

A few bars into the dance number, Terry Long stamped his foot to stop the orchestra and dancers.

Terry. at fifty, had a slim dancer's body and a biker's shaved head.

"Hello! What happened to raise the roof?" The choreographer

bounced with his palms toward the ceiling. "Am I seeing jazz hands, again Earth Princess?"

Earth Princess was a tall blonde with a runner's muscular legs and arms that moved a beat behind the music and the rest of the world. At times, she skipped a step or movement to catch up, confusing everyone on stage.

Miss Rodeo and the Harvest Queen flanked her on stage and called her "Other Left" after the first rehearsal.

Hardly looking at her, Terry shouted, "Other Left," about every eight beats.

Terry, with his back to the dancers, looked at the young orchestra conductor and pretended to put out his own eyes. "One more time."

The arms in the air movement was more uniform, but feet over lapping neighboring legs in rhythm missed the domino effect needed for twenty-two girls to look good in a line, no Rockette material here.

"Now odd numbers move up and up. Strut, Georgia Peach! This is not the Queen's walk yet. Keep up with Miss Pineapple." Terry shouted above the music.

Good luck with that, I thought. Heidi Chung was a dancer in her native Hawaii and moved with fluid rhythm. She made the simple choreography look good. What Terry Long needed was twenty-one more like Miss Pineapple.

"Good, New Roads, you've got it. Girls, watch these two and follow."

Alyce Moreaux was the Crawfish Festival Queen from New Roads, Louisiana and upstaged everybody with sheer talent. She was sassy and cool and gorgeous.

The struggling crew behind Alyce and Heidi should have been back- up dancers. But it doesn't work that way in beauty pageants.

Patrice Wilson walked on stage when Terry stopped to clap his approval to the girls for being on their marks on the last beat of the music.

Patrice was called Patsy as a child and had spent forty years becoming Patrice. She wore loose white pants and a red silk blouse that had a kimono feel. Her dark hair was braided and wrapped into a large bun at the nap of her thin neck. An antique tortoise comb held the ornate chignon in place.

"Remember, the girls get to break for spa appointments this afternoon. I'm having lunch brought in at eleven. You can use it as a break or to end rehearsal, your call."

Patrice had directed this extravaganza too long to pull rank on a frustrated, talented choreographer.

"From the top after lunch, cut by 12:30, at the latest," Terry said.

"Perfect, it's getting there, Terry. It always does. I promise you the pool and rain will stop the show."

Terry had fought the water splashing element in the short dance routine. But Patrice was driven to out-do the last show. For fourteen pageants, she had awed the audience and sponsors. Terry's ten days in Houston provided half his annual income. He created a water kicking routine worthy of a Tony nomination.

I moved away from the novice judge, Dean Ward, but was not blessed with privacy. Jamie appeared out of nowhere.

"Quite a circus, don't you think?" he said.

"Always is, but it works," I answered, still watching the stage. There were ponies and children, swings and horses being directed by young, handsome men who assisted Patrice.

One assistant, who looked more like a ball player than a stage hand, tested a swing by swinging it hard enough to touch an overhead lighting track, high above the stage.

"Jonathan!" We heard the name boom and echo in the enormous hall.

"Yes ma'am." The swinger jumped out of the swing and tied it off.

Terry Long walked down the long aisle to our seats and watched the stage activity. He gave no acknowledgement of our presence.

After the last contestant stood on a center stage point, was surrounded by running children, then exited, Terry bent down to Jamie's ear.

"You know these horses scare the shit out of me."

Jamie laughed and patted the hand on his shoulder. "I hope you don't scare it out of them tomorrow night on stage."

"There's always one. Even Patrice can't control that." Terry said

"I'm Abby Copenhaven." I extended my hand.

"I know. You were here last year in that killer blue gown," Terry said without taking or looking at my hand. I liked him, anyway.

"What will you do when the girls do the spa?" Jamie said, examining his nails and small diamond ring.

"Want to have a bite, down the street?" Terry said, still watching the stage.

"Join us, Abby?" Jamie asked. He was a gentleman.

"No thank you. I have plans."

"I'll bet you do. I saw your driver." Terry made quotation marks with his fingers. "Whew!" He fanned himself.

"He was assigned to me, that's all." My voice sounded defensive.

"Too bad." Terri walked back to the stage.

Patrice kept the show ever-changing. Patrons anticipated the artistic surprises. This year a twenty by forty-foot plexiglass rectangle saucer held eighteen inches of water to be splashed and kicked in the air by the beautiful dancers. A cascade of iridescent, oval paper pieces, lighted from above, gave the illusion of a Spring rain.

The set-up team could drain and remove the pool in three minutes, without a trace on stage for the evening gown competition.

The foyer entry to the pageant had as its centerpiece a huge plexiglass dining table, candelabrum and chairs in a square dish of water. A table cloth of flowing water completed the presentation. Patrice always gave her audience a hint of what was to come. It was her trademark, like Merle Holt's scarf on a bigger budget.

The grand budget included a white horse to open the evening gown competition. Miss Rodeo, Bea Compton, entered riding side-saddle in her white gown, then dismounted on steps of marble and wisteria.

The rehearsal continued. Classical music filled the hall. Curtains opened to a trellised garden with contestants posed on antique faux bois benches, swings and life-sized statues.

Daphne Stone and "Other-Left" held hands with a statue, a replica of their size and shape. Lighting created a scene which appeared to be an Italian painting until the girls began to move as their names were announced.

Patrice used a brief recording of each contestant's message to the audience. A few girls had to be recorded many times to get a flattering presentation of age, home and personal goals. The beauty parade flowed, while the voice of the center stage girl spoke to the audience.

Beautiful children, barefoot in long lace and linen costumes, ran to each girl with wild flowers, just as the beauty contestant stood on her star, painted on the stage floor.

The children seemed to run up the aisles to the stage randomly, one group brushed past me. Their wild, uninhibited, joyous behavior was precisely the same each time they rehearsed. One leap frogged over another exactly when the flutes joined the melody. A small, blonde boy kissed a little girl with long braids when the triangles tinkled, just before drums built up to the magical dance of a hundred children. Then, on stage, the children disappeared behind pale, billowing curtains after the flower presentation. There was an assistant dedicated only to directing the children. That young man was definite Oscar material.

The scene was fast paced and ended with a gaggle of children piled on or being pulled by white, curly-maned ponies.

Each quick appearance and disappearance of children and ponies was designed to produce audible gasps and aahhs from the audience. A listener outside the arena might guess fire works

Chapter Twenty-one

JAMIE

I looked at Jamie sitting next to me. I had seen three or four other beauty coaches already. All of them dreaded working in the same pageant with a client of Jamie's. No matter how flamboyant the beauty coaches spoke or dressed, all the hired-help pageant groomers knew they were in his shadow. Families hired them when they could not get Jamie.

Jamie's proteges had been winners in Maid of Cotton, National Lake Queen. Miss Georgia, Miss Alabama, Miss Florida, Mrs. USA, Miss Universe and too many agriculture pageants to list.

I sensed an underlayment of sadness in Jamie, even in triumphant moments.

He loved and still strived to please his mother and kindly kept his father at bay. He grew up with a father who thought a gift of a baseball glove or a football might make his young son more masculine, like his athletic brothers.

Jamie knew his father wanted to beat the girl out of him, if his mother had looked away long enough. She never did.

His two older brothers loved him and listened to his creative stories and artistic schemes. When the brothers served in the Air Force, they brought back fabrics from exotic places for Jamie to use in costume designs. They laughed at him when he began eating European style. They scrubbed his face when he tried to wear make-up.

Lonnie was six years older and gave Jamie the talk. He begged his younger brother not to put the family in a compromising position in the small Mississippi community. "Mother doesn't deserve that." Lonnie had said. "She has to know, but don't slap her in the face with it."

Lonnie could not say gay or queer in the same sentence with his baby brother's name. "You know I love you." The brothers cried.

Jamie moved away from home at eighteen. He could not live a life of pretense like his friend, Reverend Shaw.

Billy Shaw was a kind, handsome minister. He was married, had a child and was an excellent marriage counselor. He had text-book homosexual traits, that were never mentioned by family or congregation. He was simply not masculine. No one asked him to join the church soft ball team.

His wife, Olivia, let him apply her make-up. She loved this gentle, loyal man. She required almost nothing. Olivia had been abandoned as a small, homely child and now took refuge in Billy Shaw's kindness to her and a child they both claimed was his son.

Rev. Shaw remained legitimate and acceptable in his environment, despite his vague longing for another man. After all, he had a good wife, a handsome son and mowed his own yard. He baked and decorated the cakes Olivia was well known for at the church bazaars.

Jamie did not want to settle for a Rev. Shaw life.

At lunch with Terry Long, Jamie saw David Dodd for the first time. David was the pageant MC and had arrived a day late in Houston. Patrice Wilson was furious.

David looked younger than his thirty years. His neatly bearded face was so perfectly symmetrical, he could have been a photographer's model. What a shame to waste that face on a radio talk show, his sister had said.

"Terry, glad to see you. Man, you're going to have to cue me like crazy. Can I do a walk through today? I know Patrice is worried."

"No problem. She's always on somebody's case. Better yours than mine, Terry said.

"Introduce me to your friend," David shook hands with Jamie and knew they would end up together.

"Join us," Terry said. "I've got to get back. We can go over your placement while the girls are at the spa this afternoon. It's a perk Patrice wanted to give them." He shrugged his shoulders. Whether the gesture was for Jamie or the spa appointments was not clear.

"Thanks, Terry," David called after him.

"Order fancy drinks. Pageant's picking up the tab," Terry said without turning around.

"I think I need a drink," Jamie said, laughing.

They ordered dirty martinis and sat in silence a few minutes. Both knew the danger. Overt behavior that reflected private life style was not an option for either of them. People in their inner circles thought they were gay, but no one had labeled them firmly. That definite adjective attached to their names would make business dealings awkward. David aspired to be a news anchor. This was not the time to take on a partner under the spot light.

The two well-dressed men talked about their parents, growing up in small towns, pageants and pets. The pageant bought them too many martinis.

"My God, it's five o'clock," David said as he glanced at his watch. "Are you staying at the Seasons?"

"No, no room in the inn, I'm a few blocks away." Jamie had been a loner for a long time. "I have to meet my client for dinner at the hotel, though."

"Why don't you stay with me? Patrice reserved a suite, plenty of room. You might have too many martinis again." David pulled a key card from his pocket and wrote a number on its paper cover. "No expectations. Roger that?"

The key represented conflict, compromise and confrontation on so many levels. This was Texas. Jamie's family was in Mississippi.

"What the hell, over," Jamie said and put the key in his pocket.

Chapter Twenty-two

THE ELEVATOR

I tried on almost every size ten evening gown in Neiman Marcus. The sales clerk was sick of me when I finally found a size twelve, black sequined dress with long chiffon sleeves. I looked like an eight in it. "Thank you, Jesus."

"Find a pair of 9&1/2 black heels and we're in business." The sales lady was too old to stand on her feet all day, but was gracious enough to bring three pairs of evening pumps to the formal salon. One pair hurt less than the others and we settled on them. I charged $1807.22 to the Magazine's card and felt no guilt.

The hotel spa was next on my agenda. I deserved this splurge.

I called Nelle and described the cave-like atmosphere of the spa pool and the salt scrub that was too rough. An hour massage made me melt into the table. "Nelle, I think I could live like this. Love you."

The bedside phone in my room rang. "Feel like Asian, tonight?"

"Why? Do you know anybody good?" The massage had made me too relaxed.

"As a matter of fact, I do." Tom Ross was not a good impersonator. His choppy Chinese accent was so bad it was comical.

"What time?" I was laughing. He made me feel happy. Damn him."

At a world class restaurant, I spit out the sake. "Sorry. Not very lady-like, but that's terrible."

"I thought it was just me," he said. We laughed.

"I order lady something else?" Tom pressed his palms together and bowed his head.

"You sound like Hey Boy in the old *Have Gun Will Travel* series. That's a really bad accent and really out of place here."

"Please bring my wife something else, Hey Boy." The last he whispered as our server hurried to the bar.

"What is wrong with you? Do you want me to leave? Just tell me. You don't have to act like a jerk to get the message across." I was over reacting and couldn't stop.

"Was it the Hey Boy or the wife that set you off?" Tom asked. "Sorry. Just practicing on both counts. I'll stop," he said.

Our waiter brought a tall drink with what looked like a quail egg in it.

"This is going to be worse than sake. There's a little egg in my drink. What's wrong with these people?"

Tom was smiling at me. "That's a lychee nut. Try it."

"Did I ever tell you about my drink discovery at a Miss Alabama tea?"

"I want to hear all your stories."

"OK, you're over doing nice guy. There is something between jerk and boy scout. Try to hit on it."

He nodded.

"I was so hungry, I popped a big piece of divinity in my mouth and then took a swallow of Coke. That candy exploded in my mouth. Foam gushed from my nose and mouth. All the judges were at the tea. Even now, when I see divinity, I think chemical reaction."

"Did you win, anyway?"

"Of course, I did. The older I get, the better I was."

He was laughing again. I love a man who thinks I'm funny.

We tried too many Asian drinks. Most of them were too sweet for me, but Tom was determined for us to taste anything we had never had. Mai Tai, Red Lotus, Baijiu, and Shochu were the last ones I remember.

Surprisingly, we were not very intoxicated. I could be wrong, because Tom asked Hey Boy to drive us the twelve blocks back to the hotel. It was after midnight and he made it worth his while.

I was reciting no thank you in my head when we returned to the hotel.

We kissed in the elevator. A man joined us on the seventh floor. When he got off, we grabbed each other and kissed frantically. A passenger on the fourteenth floor looked at us suspiciously and got off on the sixteenth.

It was a game, now. We rode the elevator for thirty minutes, kissed and pressed our bodies on each other. We stopped and started suddenly. He held my face in his hands and I found it exciting. Finally, we got out on my floor.

"You know I want to come in," Tom said.

"You know I can't let you."

"You know there is a camera in the elevator," he said.

We hung on each other laughing. "Oh no. I'm about to wet my pants. Bye. Go. Hurry. Sorry," I said, still laughing.

I inserted my key and ran, but not fast enough.

"God, if this is an omen, I don't get it. Help me not to be stupid. You know I can be when I feel like this. That's all I got. I mean, amen."

I had talked to God, but I decided to call Nelle later.

I slept in my dress.

Chapter Twenty-three

THE JUDGES

We met with Patrice Wilson in a pale blue room with framed Audubon prints on the walls. The plush carpet had vines running through it.

The five judges were formally introduced to each other and then asked to tell something about themselves. We sat behind a semi-circle table leaving Patrice in the center, the setting for contestant interviews.

The token celebrity spoke first. Linda Levine had starred in a long running TV sitcom and now directed theater in North Carolina. She had extremely curly hair and wore a peasant blouse over a long, blue skirt.

Next, a large man of color introduced himself, James Johnson. He was neither Black, nor Indian, nor Hispanic. He may have been a perfect combination of all three. He had been an outstanding Houston Oilers quarterback and was now being groomed as a sports commentator.

James Johnson needed more grooming.

Patrice introduced Kathleen Ward. The pageant director was politely corrected.

"Dean Kathleen Ward," she smiled at the importance of her title.

"Queen Abby Copenhaven," I said and gave a royal wave. Neither the dean nor the director laughed. But the Ag commissioner and has-been quarterback made up for the women's lack of humor. I was off to a bad start.

The director explained the simple score sheet and requested we not discuss our scoring with each other or outsiders during and after the pageant.

Three judges had never been involved in a national pageant. They would need help. I would give it to them.

A list of suggested interview questions was given to each judge.

Patrice closed the meeting by saying, "Watch and listen to last year's winner and you will have a feel for what we are looking for to represent American Agriculture."

I had been a judge when Coleen Park was crowned. Patrice was right to hold her up as an example.

Silver coffee service and small almond pastries were brought in before the first interview.

"Who wants to dismiss the girls?" I asked. Blank expressions. This would be a long day. "I will, then."

The young man who was reprimanded for swinging too high on stage escorted the first contestant into the interview room, Daphne Lee Stone, Watermelon Festival Queen, Florida.

She told the judges her plans to teach deaf students and illustrated with graceful hand gestures. She was perfect.

Georgia's Peach Queen was next, Helen Epps. She was a tall blonde who smiled without reason and paused dramatically before answering the simplest question.

The Alabama Peanut Festival Queen walked in with Patrice's handsome aide, smiling at him instead of the judges. Eva Cox was beautiful, with dark hair and golden tan. She had a tiny beauty mark on her left cheek that gave her a movie star quality. Her smile and soft laughter seemed real. Her vocabulary and speech were impressive.

Mimi Norris, Maid of Cotton, was announced and hesitated in the doorway.

"Do come in." Commissioner Joel Kendrick boomed. "Tell me, does the title maid, instead of queen and princess like the other contestants bother you?"

"Not until you pointed it out," she said.

When I dismissed her, I had to ask, "Where is that question on your list, commissioner?"

"Sorry. It just popped in my head." He still had a Georgia boy accent and kind eyes, despite his ruthless political reputation.

Earth Princess, Dawn Miller, zig zagged with the young man who went too high in the swing. Both went left, then right, as he tried to exit the interview room. I wanted to shout, "Other left," but thought I had gotten off to a bad enough start.

Dairy Princess was Carolyn Weatherford, a University of Georgia student who told us more about her newly pledged sorority than herself.

Sandy McAlpine was a sunshine girl from South Florida. She had done a few orange juice commercials as the Orange Festival Queen and was well spoken. Like most of the contestants in this contest, she was tall and blonde.

Next was the pageant's first Chinese contestant, Heidi Chung from Hawaii. As the Pineapple Princess, she had her first trip to the mainland. She was smart and mature beyond her eighteen years.

The Rodeo Queen from San Antonio had a relaxed conversation with the judges, instead of an interview. Bea Comstock knew everything about rodeos and planned to breed quarter horses.

Miss Magnolia, Lee Ann Smith, interviewed well, but without energy. She was predictably tall, blonde and fit.

Annette Colberg, Corn Harvest Queen and Caroline Kirby, Cherry Festival Queen, merged in their scores and recited responses. They were pretty bookends who were over coached.

Linda Levine and Dean Ward kept to the suggested interview questions list, but the men got off on tangents half of the time.

"If you could only have one food" and "Favorite sport for males and females" were regulars. I suppose those topics were no worse than Nelle's "I am blind" favorite.

Alyce Moreaux, Crawfish Festival Queen, stepped into the room unannounced. "Are you ready for me?" she asked in the Louisiana drawl I love.

Swing Boy must have gotten side-tracked again.

"I'm from New Roads." When she finished talking about her town and the False River, we all thought about moving there. Alyce had green eyes with a thick fringe of black lashes. Her shiny, black hair was straight and swung when she walked. But it was her beautiful Bayou accent that made me want to extend her interview time.

The dean surprised us with her first comment about a contestant. "I want to talk like that."

"I want to look like that," Linda Levine said.

"I think she may be my favorite, so far," I said.

"My money is on Sanchez. Best lookin' thing I've seen in a long time," James Johnson said. "I mean, she's hot."

The dean made a zipper motion across her mouth.

"Sorry, ma'am. I forgot myself." The big football player shot me an exasperated look.

Swing Boy was back. "What's your name, son?" the commissioner asked.

"Jonathan, sir," he ducked his head. "But I'm not running this year."

The Commissioner smiled and said, "Who you got next?"

Upstate New York was home to a new pageant, Asparagus Queen. Donna O'Hare wore a green silk suit with shoes dyed to match. A little too cute, I thought.

We had a rhythm going now. All five judges fell in line to ask questions, dismiss and share a few one-line comments about each girl. The Dean was still rolling her eyes at each male interjection, but acted as though Linda Levine was holding court.

Apple Festival Queen, Toni Seagrest and her pageant best friend, Mary Beth Rollins, California Vineyard Queen seemed ordinary after the extreme beauties we couldn't stop looking at during the interviews.

From the judges' statements and facial expressions noted after each interview, I selected the winners. It was a game within the game. I had lost track of some of the mundane stats I normally collect. Tom had distracted me.

My picks were usually right, only their order sometimes scrambled. Maria Sanchez, Daphne Stone, Alyce Moreaux and Heidi Chung were the top contestants.

Only Dean Kathleen Ward had made no facial expressions and not enough prejudicial remarks for me to read her choices.

Next contestant was Beth Steinman who had a thick Maine accent. She was too thin, but delicately pretty. Beth was Cranberry Festival Queen, but refused to wear a cranberry colored dress for the interview. God bless her.

Jonathan announced Nebraska's Liz Tolbert. She made a hint of curtsy and hurried to her interview chair. The Wheat Queen wanted to be an engineer. She already had more scholarships than years she could spend in college. She allowed her naturally curly brown hair to "Do its own thing," as Linda Levine said after the interview. Huge brown eyes blinked with new contact lens. She loved math and had toured NASA, "My favorite thing about Houston," she said during her interview.

I wanted to point out how smart Liz Tolbert was. How fresh and unlike the perfect blondes in the pageant she was, but I didn't want to be hushed with the dean's zipper sign or detract from Alyce Moreaux, my first choice.

Miss Farm Beauty was a Maryland girl, Madison Conway. She was the only contestant with a major in agriculture. Her father and mother were veterinarians. The interview was beautiful, until the commissioner grilled her with questions she should have known. She stumbled on common chemical applications and went blank on agricultural economic questions.

"She's either a liar or the dumbest Ag student I've ever talked to," the commissioner said, as Swing Boy closed the door after her.

He opened the communication gate, a little late in the process. But now, we could really share our thoughts about the contestants between interviews.

"Miss Sunflower, Veronica Marcus," Jonathan said.

Veronica was a ray of California sunshine. At twenty, her confidence was a mantle that wrapped her and those near her in happiness. I smiled the whole time she was in the room. Her voice and responses to the ridiculous man-questions were kind and non-judgmental. She spoke about sports and theater with equal knowledge and enthusiasm. She played golf, tennis and softball, but did not rise to the bait James Johnson dangled to lure her into a sexist comment.

"Should we keep men and women's competition separate? Is it fair to have women's tee boxes?" he asked, re-worded and asked again.

I resented his soaking up interview time to banter his own agenda. Try that as an ABC commentator, big boy.

"I'm sorry, I lost my place. What number is that question on our sheet?" I asked.

"You think men or women are better athletes, long term?" James Johnson ignored me and continued.

Dean Ward made a slight mouth zipper gesture toward James Johnson. It was sufficient.

Veronica, the sunflower, responded, "Who can hit the ball better? Who can catch and throw it best? The ball doesn't care. Why should we?" She crossed her beautiful legs in the shortest dress in the pageant. Only Commissioner Joel Kendrick and Quarterback James Johnson saw that she wore no panties. Neither asked another unlisted interview question.

"Is she perfect for that title or what?" Linda Levine said, easing into her old sitcom character's harsh Brooklyn accent.

"We really shouldn't discuss the contestants this way," the Dean of Women said and began to shuffle forms. "But she was quite special."

The commissioner and his athletic sidekick looked at each other and said together, "Quite special."

"We want to break before we get our ducks in a row?" Linda Levine asked with a cigarette lighter already in hand.

"Won't someone be coming for the score sheets?" the dean said.

"Not if they're not here," I whispered like a naughty child. I gathered my score sheets and dropped them into my briefcase. "There, meet back in ten minutes."

No one objected. Everyone needed a restroom break after sitting through twenty-two interviews.

Of course, the very correct Dean of Women returned first, then we waited for our tardy judge.

"Should I go check on her?" the dean asked.

"She's smoking on the pool terrace, under the no smoking sign," James Johnson said. "Hey, I talked to your man in the men's room." He smiled.

"He's not my man. He's my driver, Big Boy," I said, too harshly. I hope I don't have to make this man cry in front of everybody.

"No offense meant," he said. "Are we done here?"

"Good man, Tom Ross," the commissioner said.

"Are we talking about the same man?" I asked without looking up.

"Good man to have on your side, hell of a lawyer." His friend did not defend him as a good man, bad sign.

Linda Levine rushed in, out of breath and reeking of cigarette smoke. "Sorry, I was talking to the most interesting man," she said with a girlish smile.

The commissioner and ex-jock shot amused looks at me. They were fanning the bitch flame. Were they brave or stupid?

"Dean Ward, will you add each girl's interview score and tell us the results? That way, we know what we're going into tonight. Everybody OK with that?" I spoke standing, the other four judges were seated. I hummed *"That's the way, uhuh, uhuh, I like it."*

"Wait. I don't think I scored two of the girls," Linda Levine said.

"Pull out any blank forms when you get to them." I instructed the dean.

Now, with a job, she was all business. "Three blank sheets." She said with a hard look at our celebrity judge. "Here," Dean Ward handed the three sheets to Linda. "Can you remember them?"

"If I can't, they must not have been very impressive, so I'll just put a two on each one." Linda Levine spoke casually.

With one cruel, unsympathetic, cigarette breath, she sealed the fate of three girls with high expectations. Three girls with new gowns and families in the audience. I didn't know who the three were and I was glad.

"These scores are really polarized," the dean said. She pushed her tally sheet out on the table. She had wonderful hand writing, almost calligraphy.

At the top were five girls who scored twenty-two to twenty-three. On the bottom of the list were ten girls who scored below fifteen. There were seven names in the middle of the list with totals of nineteen to twenty-one.

"The haves and the have nots," Linda Levine said dramatically.

"We each need a copy of that," I said. The raw scores will be collected shortly."

The matronly dean went to work. Her chubby fingers, which had never been graced by a wedding ring, moved, pen in hand, like a fast machine.

The copies had pageant numbers only. She knew a thing or two about privacy.

I was happy to note my favorite, Alyce Moreaux, had scored a twenty-three. Probably two judges gave her a four and three of us scored fives on her interview. I tried to do the hypothetical math for overview and entertainment.

A soft knock interrupted my calculations. The door opened slowly. "Mrs. Wilson requests all your score sheets in this envelope. Please seal it," Swing Boy, now in a light gray suit, said formally. He was trying to ease back into good graces with the director.

The good Dean of Women turned the copies face down casually. I liked her better. I needed to call Nelle again and recant my criticism of her as a judge.

"Good timing," James Johnson said, now standing next to me. "Your driver asked me to join you for lunch." He looked down at me with a smirk. God, he was big.

The commissioner stood. "You know Tom and I are old friends. I thought we might let him wine and dine us a little while we're here. That boy knows where to go."

"Tom? Tom Ross?" Linda Levine stood up now, gathering a crafty, fringed purse that was far too big for her. "He's your driver? I thought he was an attorney." Her penciled eyebrows raised.

"He is and a fine one. We're just having fun with Miss Abby. She's had a little run-in with him." The commissioner smiled.

They had talked. "Why didn't you just write my name on the bathroom wall while you were in there?" I snapped.

"You can sit by me, Abby," The dean offered, taking my side against a pair of macho on-lookers and a jealous celebrity.

"Thank you, Kathleen." I dared to omit the Dean title and it was accepted.

The commissioner took his own car and offered a ride to Linda Levine and James Johnson. Linda said she was riding with my driver. Joel and James walked her to the black Mercedes.

I quickly put Dean Ward in the front seat. She talked to Tom non-stop for the two-mile ride to a small, elegant Tex-Mex restaurant.

Tom parked and opened Linda Levine's door. "I promise, best you've ever had," he said.

"I'll bet." Getting out of the back seat, she looked at her feet, then up at his eyes. I could see she was in trouble.

He opened my door last. Why did I allow him the pleasure? I should have gotten out unaided and beaten them all to the restaurant. My manners were getting like Tamsey's. Stop.

The smell of frying onions, peppers and roasting meat greeted us as we entered. James Johnson and Joel Kendrick were already seated at a round table for six.

"How did they get here so fast?" I asked.

"Better driver," Tom replied and I laughed without meaning to.

"I'm glad you didn't go too fast," The dean chimed in, as he pulled her chair out.

The commissioner nudged James Johnson to stand up when we came to the table. Yes, he needed a lot more grooming.

A striking woman with a long, black braid put chips and several bowls of salsas on the table. The corn chips were almost transparent and still warm from the fryer.

"We'd like queso," Tom said to her and she hurried to the open kitchen.

"I like a kitchen you can watch," Linda Levine said, looking at Tom. "It's like watching a small drama. You can see everyone's role."

"I don't think I've ever dined where I can actually see the cooks," Dean Ward said. "I may like just being served better."

"How about you, Abby?" Tom asked.

"Oh, I just cook at home, when I'm not sewing my own clothes." No one laughed.

Everyone was cordial. Why did I need to be sarcastic? Tom, it was Tom's fault for herding me, controlling my time, making me vulnerable. I could be resting in my room, right now, ordering room service instead of vying for salsa between two big, hungry men.

"I'm a lefty. I'll try not to bump you while we eat," James Johnson said.

"A pitcher of margaritas," Tom said quietly to our server.

"Thank you, Jesus," I said.

"Is that our blessing?" Linda Levine quipped.

"It can be," Dean Ward answered for me.

I tried not to look at Tom. I had to go home in the morning and not do anything stupid tonight. I knew what he was. Maybe everybody at the table did. No thank you, no thank you.

Small trays of artistically presented food began to flood our table. Vegetable plates too perfect to eat, tiny roasted chops with baked fruit, layered dishes with sauces, pastry triangles filled with strong cheese, and bite-sized tamales.

"I'm a vegetarian," Linda Levine announced. No one cared. We were enamored by the beautiful food.

"Is there anything better than this?" I asked.

"Maybe not," the dean said, laughing a little.

"What can I eat? I don't know what any of this is." Linda Levine was upset. She needed a cigarette, since Tom had asked her not to smoke in the car. She was hungry and disappointed in Tom's lack of response to her celebrity status.

The dean came to her rescue. She began making a plate for the diva. "Cheese pastry, fruit, fried vegetables, layered avocado, lettuce, beans, sour cream, there." She passed the plate, not as pretty as it had been, to Linda Levine.

"Thank you," she sniffed.

I ate a few bites of everything except the squid, poached, not fried and surrounded with an inky colored sauce.

Tom gave a subtle salute with his fork in my direction each time he was impressed with a taste. I followed suit, trusting his palate more each time. We liked the same foods. Nelle would have said, "What's not to like? You're in the best Mexican restaurant in America."

"I had a feeling you would like this place," Tom said, looking at me across the table.

"We like it too, Tom," the commissioner said. "Of course, it's not in the same category as that little café in Laredo."

They both laughed and shook their heads. "God, we were sick," Tom said and poured Linda Levine another margarita. Dean Ward put her hand over her glass.

"Bernard was the worst. We had to take him to an emergency room." Tom was suddenly silent. He answered the question posed by the dean's cocked head and sad eyes. "He died a few years ago, my best friend, best man in my wedding."

"Which one?" The commissioner laughed, trying to shift the mood. Immediately, he regretted his remark, looked down at his plate and mouthed, "shit."

I looked at Tom with raised eyebrows and lowered opinion.

"Dessert, anybody?" Tom said to break the tension at the table.

When no one else accepted, Kathleen Ward finally said, "No thank you." She was disappointed.

I rode back to the hotel in the front seat. The commissioner had herded the other judges into his car with a slight nod to Tom.

"I'll be waiting for you after the pageant," Tom said.

"I don't need a driver. The Pageant is right here." I avoided his face.

"You may want a late dinner," he said as he parked in the reception area and opened my door. "Don't throw me away. You mean something to me and I don't want to lose you. This might be our last chance." He touched my shoulder and got back into the car.

He was good. I was about to cry. Maybe I was crying. Damn him. By the time I reached the elevator, I had myself worked up again. I bet the commissioner and James Johnson thought I was sleeping with him, like everybody else.

In the elevator, I wondered, how many marriages? How many affairs, live-ins, lies? No, thank you. No, thank you.

Now I knew I was crying. Tom was like my Santa Fe cowboy in a tux. What a waste. I needed one of them to be the one.

Chapter Twenty-four

ENTERTAINMENT

I slipped on the black dress from Neiman Marcus and felt good about tonight. Patrice warned us that the swim suit competition was fast, with no final parade. I agreed that the lining up and turning back sides to the audience had a little livestock sale feel. She did not exaggerate about the whirlwind presentation. I was not prepared.

A Ferris wheel with clear platforms where metal seats should be, faced the audience. The huge wheel was all white lights. It lowered one standing beauty at a time to center stage. The contestant walked either left or right to a floral swing which moved out over the audience and returned without the girl.

The rhythm of the sparkling Ferris wheel, the swings and the music made a graceful swirl of movement on stage. Twenty-two girls in less than twenty- three minutes.

I did not have time to write any comments on the score sheets, only a quick 1-5 score at the bottom. There was no time to fish out Dean Ward's carefully copied interview sheets. What was good entertainment did not facilitate good judging. I wrote big fives on ten sheets, those girls I anticipated being in the top ten. All the contestants were fives and fours in swim suits.

The big quarterback was struggling to score and had gotten a contestant behind. I pushed each of my sheets toward James Johnson, to my left. He must have cheated a lot in school. He was good at it. As far as I could tell, he imitated my scores exactly.

At least I know two of us gave fives to the same girls. No, better than that. Linda Levine was back, late. The competition had started without her. I smelled her cigarette trail pass behind me before I saw her. She quickly checked James Johnson's sheets and nodded to him.

Almost certainly, the ten would be Maria Sanchez, Heidi Chung, Daphne Lee Stone, Alyce Moreaux, Mary Ann Rollins, Veronica Marcus, Bea Comstock, Eva Cox, Lee Ann Smith and Beth Steinman. I am good at what I do. Only Linda's inexcusable, two-point scores worried me.

The last Ferris wheel ride was saved for Coleen Park, reigning American Agriculture Queen. Her crown was seven inches tall, but appeared to be worn comfortably. A fitted, white beaded gown gave the platinum blonde a dream-like stage presence. She pointed to the orchestra. The wild applause stopped and the music started. Coleen Park sang.

I remembered Becky Alford's voice at the Watermelon Festival pageant and got ready for mediocre. After all, this was not a talent contest.

Coleen sang *Girl from Ipanema* and moved very little from center stage. I wondered if the song was pre-recorded, as the speeches had been. No, she was too perfect. There was a lazy, raspy quality in her voice that the song needed. She sang effortlessly.

Curtains closed between the singer and the huge, lighted wheel. When she finished her song, a cascade of tiny, clear balloons fell on and around her. When they stopped, she had disappeared. The audience was spell bound, leaving a long pause before breaking into stadium level cheering.

Her song and applause had given the director's crew enough time to set up the water feature for Terry Long's anticipated dance number.

David Dodd was impressive in a tuxedo. His long, messy hair, which had no bearing on his radio talk show, was slicked back like an Italian movie star. Unfortunately, he was a card reader, but his voice made up for his lack of stage presence. He gave credit to volunteers, the director, choreographer, set designer, and finally the judges.

We were introduced and given routine applause. No one cared who we were. It was the Patrice Wilson Extravaganza and the beauty queens they had come to see.

David Dodd gave a conductor's arm gesture to que the orchestra.

Curtains opened to a chorus line moving toward the audience with arms up, palms to the ceiling, pumping rhythm like a drum. One line back. One line up, too fast to see any imperfections in uniformity.

The dancers made big, round-house kicks over each other's steps before jumping in the shallow pool of water. The pool was invisible to the audience until the wild splashing began. High kicks and straight arm dips to floor level sprayed water dramatically. Suddenly, a cascade of paper rain and sparkling light covered the girls. Then they were gone. Curtains closed.

Not one of us made a note during the three -minute dance routine. How could Patrice Wilson top this for the evening gown competition? No wonder she was no longer called Patsy.

I looked for Tom when the house lights came up. Brief intermission, less than ten minutes.

Linda Levine disappeared with the contestants. She needed a cigarette, and the smoking area was at the far end of the building.

I didn't have to look far for Tom. A server in black put two pitchers and five glasses on the judges table. Tom stood behind him. I knew this was not water.

"Thank you, Jesus," I whispered.

Poor Dean Ward. She held her hand over her glass at lunch. Maybe she won't be thirsty. Maybe she didn't drink during the day. Maybe I'll drink hers.

Tom Ross slipped a small note in my hand, "French tonight." I hoped he meant cuisine, I think. I liked his hand writing, small and square, with no flair.

The evening gown sequence was like a scene from an eerie movie. White horses, children in white, waterfalls, wild flowers, and girls posed as still life paintings. Classical music created a hush over the usually talkative audience. The voice-over while each contestant moved away from her pose was dramatic. The gowns were spectacular.

Again, not enough time to score. I wrote only a large number on each sheet. I noted James Johnson had stepped out with a few scores which did not match mine. Only Maria Sanchez received his highest score in the evening gown competition.

Maria's pale aqua gown made her dark skin glow under the

lights. She had a sexy, graceful walk that only dancers have. The big quarterback was right. She was hot.

Like James Johnson, I gave my number one choice a five and all the others a four or three.

Alyce Moreaux was a contrast on every level to the wall to wall, predictable beauties. Her heavy, straight dark hair and slightly devilish self-confidence were refreshing.

Alyce's pose on stage was not advantageous, but she made the best of a frozen, bent position, looking into a mirror pool. The light that reflected on her face was wonderful. God really makes beautiful women.

Her gown was full-skirted and ankle length, smacking of Swan Lake. The waist and bodice were tight, exaggerating small waist and pushed-up breasts. The look worked for her.

I could not second guess Dean Kathleen Ward or Commissioner Kendrick, but I was betting they voted for wholesome, predictable candidates. Rodeo Queen, Miss Sunflower and Watermelon Queen were their speed.

Linda Levine might support the only Jewish girl in the pageant or liberal-out and champion ethnic beauties like Heidi Chung or Maria Sanchez. It was hard to know.

There was not a girl on stage who could not be a winner. Only Linda Levine's random low interview scores put a stick in the spokes. She could not be forgiven for her casual low-balling to excuse losing track of girls so similar. What did she expect? A beauty pageant in America has tall, smiling blondes, lots of them.

I saw Jamie standing at the end of his row, watching the stage. His client sat next to the aisle seat. She was nervous and dabbed at the corners of her eyes. He put his hand on her shoulder. They had spent a lot of time and money together.

Swing Boy appeared in the roped off space between judges' table and stage. "Mother, uh, Mrs. Wilson," he stammered, "Wants to collect your ballots, I mean score sheets." He opened a large, gold envelope to receive 110 score sheets. Patrice Wilson would be disappointed when her tally committee saw only a number on the score sheets with no comments.

"Wait, I have one sheet left," Linda Levine said.

"Mayday. Mayday," James Johnson said.

"Houston, we have a problem," the commissioner added.

Dean Ward jerked Linda's stack of sheets from her without a word. She counted 21, then placed them in numerical order.

"Number one is missing." The dean spoke directly to me. We were in charge. Alpha will out.

"Who was number one?" The sitcom celebrity asked softly.

"Daphne Stone, Watermelon Queen," the commissioner whispered. "And don't do any of that low scoring mess because you can't get your shit together."

Linda Levine looked at the red face of the Commissioner of Agriculture and back at the Dean of Women and put a big five on her sheet. She pushed the stack to Jonathan.

Did I see a nod between the dean and the commissioner?

The MC raved about the bounty of awards that winner and runners-up would receive. Those who were intimate with this silent giant of a pageant knew his impressive list was a token. Loot was usually over 100,000. for the queen, not including travel expenses and scholarships. Cash and gifts of twenty to thirty thousand was traditional for the runners-up. A new car was sometimes "thrown in" by a sponsor for a few commercials.

The commissioner smiled at me. "Good crop this year. Can you do it next time? You're good, you know."

"I have a problem with Tom Ross," I said without turning my head.

"He's part of why you're here."

"I know that now, but I can't let myself get tangled up with him. I've been too straight, too long."

"I understand, but he may need some straight. Most of us do."

David Dodd returned to the stage with Coleen Park. The audience applauded for several minutes. "Somehow, our judges have selected the top ten," David said in his melodious radio voice.

I glanced behind me for Tom Ross. I had to let him know I was not meeting him tonight and was leaving on an earlier flight in the morning. No need for him to drive me. I had rehearsed the two-line rejection several times. It never got better.

Instead of Tom, I saw Jamie watching David Dodd on stage. As

David read the top ten names and their titles, the girls walked onto the stage and sat in enormous, Alice in Wonderland styled wing-back chairs.

"Second runner- up, Maria Sanchez." Maria jumped out of her chair and started throwing kisses to her parents in the audience. They were crying and so was she. She had just changed their lives.

James Johnson clapped longer than he should have.

"First runner-up," I heard blah, blah, blah, Alyce Moreaux." She bowed from the waist, like a ballerina, and accepted her giant bouquet of Texas wild flowers.

Coleen Park lifted the huge crown from her head and held it aloft like a fighter's championship belt. The applause was deafening.

I saw Tom and held my hand out to him in a stop gesture.

"The 1985 National Agriculture Queen is Daphne Lee Stone." David Dodd shouted over the crowd.

Daphne rose and glided forward, bending slightly to receive her banner and crown. Daphne and Coleen could have been sisters under the lights. If I squinted my eyes, they were twins.

I looked at the dean and the commissioner. They could not have grinned any bigger. They stood and hugged each other.

Linda Levine remained seated, tears in her eyes. She had her hopes on Miss Pineapple, Heidi Chung.

I made a bee line for the lobby elevator. I was crying, too.

The orchestra played. David Dodd and Jamie pointed at each other and smiled. Jamie had done it again, or so his client and admirers thought. His bonus would be spent on David, his new friend.

In the calm, coolness of my room, I called Nelle. She listened to the pageant results, judges' roles, rant on Linda Levine and my sobs.

"I'm afraid of being alone forever and I am sick to death of being a good woman, a role model, whatever the hell you want to call whatever I am. Is it worth it?"

"In the long run, yes." Nelle's voice was soft. She was so wise.

"Thank you," I whispered. I loved Nelle Ashford.

Chapter Twenty-Five

GOOD ADVICE

Tom stood beside his old friend, the commissioner, who was still clapping.

"I had a long day in court. Want to get a drink?" Tom said.

"Sure. And a little supper. You know she's not coming," the commissioner said.

"Yeah, I guess I do."

They had burgers and beer served at the hotel bar.

"Only way an old dog like you can get a woman like Abby is with an act of God. He's got to give both of you a sign," the commissioner said, finishing his second beer.

"Pity to passion in a few steps. You've got to be patient. A burnt child fears the fire. Listen to me and look for a sign. Promise me you're going to do her right. You hear me? Make it happen. Hell, you know how to do that."

"I think she's too afraid of what I've been, things I've done," Tom said, running his finger around the rim of an untouched beer.

"Be the big brother she never had, the daddy she wanted, the knight who puts her on a pedestal." The commissioner gestured with his empty glass.

"That's crazy. She's too smart for games."

"Good women are different. Maybe you just haven't had one, yet. They might act sassy and self-sufficient and mainly, they are, but they still feel they need us. God bless 'em."

Tom stood up.

"Sit down. This advice is gold and I haven't ever given it away. I think Abby's worth it. You're worth it. You let her walk and you'll never feel the same about anything. Did you mean it, when you told me she was it?"

Tom Ross sat back on his stool and ordered another beer. "Take this one away. It's had too much hot air on it."

"A good woman is so kind, deep down, she doesn't want to hurt or disappoint you. She'll give you another chance, and another." The commissioner laughed, remembering the learning curve with his wife of thirty-five years.

"You can buy a woman's loyalty and attention, but you don't want that."

"Never have. Gets old," Tom said.

"Always does," the commissioner said.

"Do anything you can for her and her family. Good women are big on family."

"I love her, Joel. She's it."

"If you want a looker who'll love the kids, feed your dog and jerk a knot in your tail when you need it, you gotta work for it. Every time you have a choice, do right. That's all I'm sayin'."

"I made a fool out of myself with that Candace thing. She doesn't trust me. I don't blame her."

"I heard all about that mess," the commissioner grimaced.

"Really?" Tom was surprised.

"Old Hiram Wilson said you nailed another judge for good measure. Said her husband almost caught you. Good God, man. You get a shot at a woman like Abby once in a lifetime. Do right." The commissioner put a hundred- dollar bill on the bar, slapped Tom on the back and started to walk away. He turned back to Tom. "Look for a sign."

A hotel shuttle took me to the airport at 5:30 am. There was one other passenger, an old lady who had three red suitcases.

I cried when we left Houston. I tried to think about the pageant's outcome, or make some brilliant deduction about recognizing ethnic beauty and traditional beauty. I thought about James Johnson and Linda Levine, Maria Sanchez and Heidi Chung and the commissioner and Dean Ward and Daphne Stone. It was all a jumble.

Were the red suitcases an omen? Stop it. What's wrong with you?

I began to cry again.

"Did you lose somebody, Honey?" the elderly lady asked.

"Yes, yes I did." I leaned back and stopped my tears. It is a blessing and a curse to be an alpha female.

On the short flight to Birmingham, I was sure being a good woman was the hardest thing I'd ever done.

Another country song in the making,

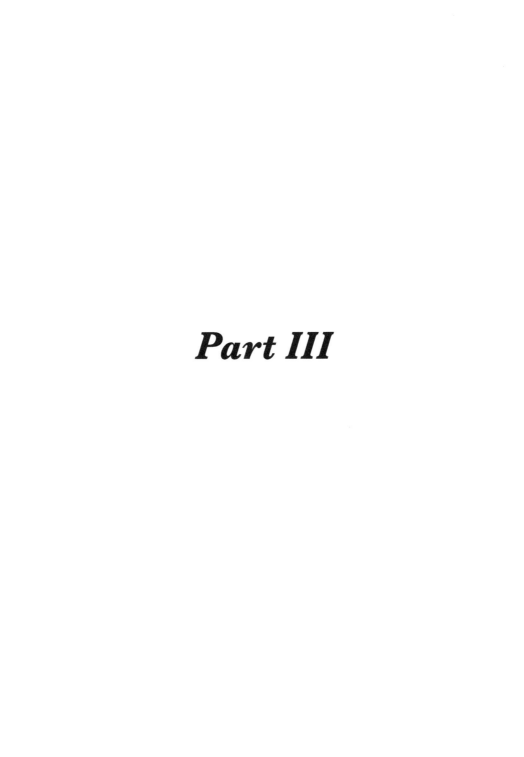

Part III

Chapter Twenty-six

Birmingham traffic was sluggish, but at least the airport taxi was moving. "Going to be almost a hundred degrees today. Hard to keep this old cab cool," the young driver said. The thirty-minute drive from airport to home gave me time to think. I needed to water my plants and pick up V. I was always glad to return to the brick townhouse that was home now. Funny, I never missed the big house sold during the divorce.

I knew this was my place when I first saw the neglected garden in the walled courtyard. The over grown remnants of a master gardener's talent were still there. Espaliered fruit trees, an antique iron arbor and an empty koi pond made me ready to make the realtor an offer on the neglected, over-priced property, before we walked inside.

"It's the location that makes this place so pricey," The middle-aged realtor had said. "This is the only one of the six townhouses that is separated and has a garden."

The floors on the first level were brick laid in a herringbone pattern. The big kitchen had a view of the garden through a floor to ceiling window, which I guessed was once a dining area. There was a foyer, a study, half bath and a large living room with a brick fireplace. This place was a ten-minute drive to my office. It had bearing fruit trees. I would make preserves. My nesting genes were on fire. I was already placing my furniture before we walked upstairs to see three bedrooms and two bathrooms.

The taxi cab driver carried my luggage to the front door and I paid him. "Thank you. I don't need any change."

As he drove away, I fished in my small travel purse for keys. I reminded myself of Nelle, but with a smaller purse. No keys. "I am losing my mind." And sweating in the morning sun as I lose it. Ida had a key, but I hated to call her at work. I didn't want my office to know I was home until tomorrow.

"Back window." I dropped my carry-on bag and purse on top of my suitcase to walk to the garden gate. I had never been able to lock the high window in the back which gave light to the stairwell. The old architectural element had been added and could still be opened. One of my daughters made the discovery last Christmas, when she lost her key.

Access to the window required a short climb on an ornate wooden trellis. "No problem," I said to myself, a self who had no idea of age, weight or coordination.

My right foot broke through the wood as I reached the top. I fell, pulling the trellis to the ground with me. My foot was turned at an impossible angle, still wedged in the wooden design. I was sweating profusely.

"Ellen, Ellen!" I called as loudly as I could to my neighbor. "Please be home," I whispered. My foot was hurting badly. I dared not move it. "Ellen, Ellen Youngblood!" I shouted her name over and over, until my throat was dry and sore. She must be at the grocery store. Maybe she took her elderly father with her.

Old Sidney Youngblood was ninety-three and dependent on her. Although he seemed physically able to do things, he was emotionally and socially isolated. He begged to go anywhere with anybody he saw. He was desperate to get out of the house and be with people. Unfortunately, Ellen, at sixty-five, was a loner, except for a few church activities.

"Ellen, Ellen!" I screamed.

No one would check on me until tomorrow afternoon, when Ida would return V. I thought about getting to the hose for water, but my first move rendered me paralyzed with pain.

There was a shadow over me. "Mr. Youngblood, couldn't you hear me screaming?"

"I heard you, but you wasn't calling me and Ellen's not here. She's at a retreat 'til in the morning. I'm glad you're home, I'm out of milk for my cereal." The thin, old man in a winter plaid shirt, leaned over me.

"Mr. Youngblood, I'm injured. I need you to help me. Call an ambulance or just 911. Can you do that?" I spoke slowly. I was cooking in the sun. "Can you get me a drink of water?"

"In the war, I knew what to do. We wrapped an injured man in blankets, so he wouldn't go into shock 'til the medics could get to him. My outfit was in Germany. Coldest I've ever been. Sometimes we would stand behind the idling tanks all night to stay warm. I can help you."

"No, Mr. Youngblood. Just call for help," I said. "Please."

He was gone. There was no one else. "Please, Jesus, let him come back."

He wrapped me in an antique, double wedding ring quilt, carefully tucking the edges under me. I did not resist, it was too painful. My hair was wet. My eyes were stinging with salt and sun.

"Please, Mr. Youngblood, call 911 on the wall phone in your kitchen. Tell the men where to come. Hurry."

He left again. The next sound I heard was a siren, then men talking in front of the townhouse. I heard doors slamming shut. I screamed. "Help. Somebody help me!"

Two young EMT's came running through the garden gate. "We thought Mr. Youngblood was our patient. He's in the ambulance." The men looked at each other and blew out deep breaths. "Hang on lady. Let's get that foot immobilized."

The young men gave me water, removed the quilt and trellis and asked a string of questions. Then I was in the cool ambulance. Mr. Youngblood refused to get out.

"I'm here alone. I have to go with my daughter. She needs me." The old man held on to my gurney and pleaded with the young men in the ambulance. "I'm a retired doctor, you know. Want me to take her vital signs?" he said in a stronger voice than I had ever heard from him.

"Please, no," I said. "I can't take much more of his first aid."

"We've got it, Doc." The EMT's were wonderful. They even retrieved my bags and purse.

After emptying my purse to find identification and insurance cards,

I was admitted to the emergency room of the hospital. I was x-rayed, given a shot and had another IV started.

In my absence, Mr. Youngblood bragged to anyone in the waiting room who would listen, that he had saved my life. "Like riding a bicycle, it came right back to me." he repeated.

A teaching nurse, with her gaggle of nursing students from the near-by Junior College, stood in the emergency room waiting area. The teacher asked for volunteers to have their blood pressure taken by student nurses.

Sidney Youngblood stood up, announcing, "I practiced medicine for half a century. Too old now. I'll be your guinea pig." He laughed a masculine laugh. He was no longer a child in his daughter's household. He sounded like a man to be respected here.

The teacher demonstrated to a small circle of students how to start an IV in an unconscious patient, while three of her students took blood pressure readings from volunteers.

"Miss Fuller, Miss Fuller," a pretty black student, Precious Johnson, said to interrupt her teacher's instruction.

"Not now, Precious. Can't you see I'm busy."

"OK." Precious walked back to Mr. Youngblood, lying on a gurney.

"Miss Fuller, Miss Fuller," she tried again.

"What is it?" her teacher said through clenched teeth.

"Sorry to bother you and all, but I thank my patient dead."

And he was. A circus of nurses and administrators filled the small ER with clip boards and worry wrinkles.

Six hours after arrival, my fractured foot was set and put in an awkward boot. I was released from the hospital. I called my daughter Sara, a set designer in Atlanta.

"Leave me a message."

So, I did. "I'm at Saint Vincent's Hospital with a broken foot, can't drive for six to eight weeks, I need some help. Bring your key. Can you come right away?"

Next, I called Ida's home number. Another recording. Maybe she was still camping. I didn't leave a message.

I adjusted my position in the wheel chair and propped my foot up on a plastic chair in the waiting room. My right foot was starting to hurt again.

"What do you want us to do with your father?" an orderly was sent to ask me.

"He's not my Father. He is, was, my neighbor. His daughter is on a church retreat and can't be contacted until tomorrow. By the way, I need something to eat."

"Can you give me more information?" the young orderly asked.

"Can you get me a hamburger and Coke from the cafeteria?" I imitated his nasal, fast speech.

He started to leave, then at a signal from the admitting nurse, rolled me to her desk phone. It was Sara. "So sorry about your foot, how did it happen?" She did not allow me enough time to tell her the details. "Is there any way I can use your car, if you can't drive for a couple of months? It would really help Ken and me out."

"What? I'm asking you to help me, Sara. Are you hearing me?" I hovered between screaming and crying.

"Mother, you don't understand. I have to take him to class every morning before I can go to work. You know Atlanta traffic. Sorry, he can't afford a car."

"Is this Ken staying with you? Does your father know? What is he bringing to the table? No, no, he can't use my car. I don't think I need to contribute to this kind of situation. By the way, I'm sitting in the waiting room, you know, waiting."

"Daddy's right about you. Count out that money, make sure everything's equal and fair. Everything has to be your way. Everything has to be proper. You won't even let us have the river house. Do you have any idea how that much money would help us? But it's all about you. You can't use the car, you don't use the river house, but you don't want anybody else to have them. Thanks a lot!" Sara hung up.

"Want to come get your mother at the hospital? Guess not." I felt alone and weepy.

Nelle was on a rare vacation with her family at the Cloister. Her husband and Hunter played golf in an annual Sea Island charity tournament. She would come. I would not call her.

Millicent, baby daughter, had just opened a small restaurant in

Nashville, with a partner, Michael Moore. Michael was a *build it, they will come* chef with almost no business sense. Millicent shocked everyone by hiring Mustafa, a Moroccan pastry chef from a cruise line, to run the small kitchen.

"Hell no. I can't work with anybody you pull off the street. He might not even be legal." Michael had yelled.

"He's legal."

"You mean lethal. Did you see that big knife he carries?"

"Maybe we won't get robbed," Millicent said. "He's hired."

"I trust you. I'm just nervous about getting open and really making it. This is the last of my trust fund money," Michael said. He put his arms around Millicent.

"He can make anything and he has experience and costs very little," Millicent argued with her business partner and ducked away from his arm. "You've got to have variety and back-up. Get over yourself. Any cook can do what you do in the kitchen, but faster. You can learn from Mustafa."

They argued, but I saw the looks between them. He allowed Millicent to manage and became comfortable with her ability when the rave reviews and bank statements came.

Millicent met identical twins working in a bar-b-que restaurant and talked them into being the wait staff. All the pretty, thirty-two-year olds had ever known was waiting tables. Molly and Margaret wore oversized football jerseys over jeans most of the time and were always pleasant and efficient. They had matching black ponytails and when stressed, still spoke their own language to each other.

Millicent's last contested hire was Leshaun Lee, who had been fired from a fast food chain for being a clean freak. He was fast and brilliant. In a few days, he was a good bartender. He was soon affectionately called Lee Lee by the twins, then everyone. Many came for his special concoctions and his huge smile.

What a crazy good time we had decorating the small restaurant on a tight budget. I had enjoyed working as a team with Millicent and her staff. I took a week's vacation from the magazine and slept on her apartment couch. We pulled all-nighters, painted wall murals and made calligraphy menus. Maybe she could come for a few days.

"Mother, I can't take any time off. Not even a shift. And now, Michael and Lee Lee have flu. I'm bartending and Mustafa's doing everything in the kitchen. Molly and Margaret are plating and garnishing before they serve. I don't know how it's getting done. Senator Bailey's daughter has a party here tomorrow. We'll have to work through the night here to be ready."

"So sorry about your poor foot. You'll figure it out, Mother. You always do. Love you." Millicent's response was kinder, but no more helpful than Sara's.

"Can we have information on the elderly man who came with you? We have to make arrangements, it's been eight hours, now." The charge nurse said.

"You will have to figure it out," I said.

"Here is your hamburger and Coke." The orderly put a plastic tray in my lap. He had brought extra napkins and ketchup. "Thank you, Jesus."

"You know you're dismissed from the hospital, don't you, Mrs. Copenhaven? May we call your husband to come and get you?" The efficient little charge nurse said. "My daughter works in his office. I can call him for you, if you like."

"I don't have a husband, but I think I still have a driver."

I called Tom. His card was in my small, travel purse. I have no idea how it got there. "I need a driver."

"I hoped you would."

I told him about the key and trellis and fall and neighbor and EMT's and daughters. I was sobbing when I finished.

"Let me speak to your nurse, please," Tom said. Without comment, I handed the desk phone receiver back to the nurse who seemed to be running the waiting room.

After a two-minute conversation, with nods and "I understand," repeated many times, she had me wheeled to a private room, where an aide bathed and dressed me in a hospital gown. A young nurse on the floor brought a pain pill and promised to help me put on clothes from my suitcase in ten hours, when my attorney and driver were scheduled to arrive.

"Until then, rest. I'll check on you," she said politely.

What could Tom Ross have promised or threatened to make this happen? I didn't care. I went to sleep.

Tom had a pillow and a blanket in his back seat. He and a nurse moved me from wheel chair to car.

"Did you drive all night?" I asked, embarrassed for him to see me without makeup.

"We'll be back in Texas by midnight tonight. What do you need before we leave?" He put my suitcase in his trunk.

"I need to go home."

"Let's worry your girls a little. Be out of pocket. I have Bernice waiting at my house to take care of you. I swear I'll get you back the day you want to go. Let me do this for you."

"Can't you stay here a few days?" What was I saying?

"I'm in the middle of the biggest case my firm has ever had. My staff and I have been able to direct everything by fax and phone until now. The next two weeks will be show time in Judge Moreno's courtroom and Judge Moreno don't play."

"I'm too tired to fight you. Drive me home to pack." My thoughts raced ahead. I hoped I had left the townhouse clean.

Together we hobbled to the front door. "I'm crazy. We still don't have a key," I said, sitting on the concrete bench near the front door. "Can a person die from exhaustion?"

Tom took a credit card from his wallet, wedged it between lock and door jam and pushed the door open.

"That makes me feel safe," I said.

We struggled to a slip covered couch. I was out of breath with the effort. "Go upstairs and get under clothes, pajamas, a few blouses, whatever you see. I have some things in my suitcase, if I can do laundry at your house." He was up the steps before I could finish.

"Bernice will take care of everything, you'll see," he called down the staircase.

I yelled, "Just empty a couple of drawers into a suitcase or two, and don't look."

"I love a detail oriented woman. At least I don't need to worry about you being OCD."

"OC what?" I felt dizzy.

"No night gowns? I didn't peg you for a pajama girl." He was carrying two suitcases downstairs.

"A robe?" I asked.

"Of course."

"I love your draperies and Persian rugs. They look old. The rugs, not the drapes." He walked to the car with the luggage.

For the first time since we dragged ourselves through the front door, Tom stopped and looked around. He walked to the kitchen and brought a diet coke to me. "I really like your taste. It feels European, without being fancy or fussy. Whatever look this is, I want some of it. It's elegant and comfortable at the same time."

"You're sure you're not gay?" We laughed together.

"One last favor, a friend kept my dog while I was in Texas. V has to come with us. I have to warn you, she's a big girl."

"I like big girls, let's go pick her up." Tom pulled me upright and put my arm over his shoulder. It was awkward, but took pressure off my foot. We were not pretty getting to the car.

"Didn't they give you any crutches?"

"It was after I spoke to Sara and I think I threw them somewhere," I said. He might as well know the dark side.

Ida met us outside her apartment with V on a leash. Dog bag and bowls were neatly packed. She stared at Tom shamelessly.

"You weren't kidding. What breed is she?" Tom asked.

"She's a Bernese Mountain dog, Swiss originally, about a hundred pounds." I was used to identifying her to people.

When Tom put V's things in the trunk, Ida gave me a silent, wide mouthed scream. "He's so hot. Never come back," she whispered.

I thanked her and asked for secrecy. My foot started to ache. V tried to lie down on me in the back seat. It took both Ida and Tom to beg and drag her into the front seat. For a long time, she kept her big head on the center console to watch me. Finally, she fell asleep and put her head in Tom's lap.

Chapter Twenty-Seven

ALPHA FEMALES

"Good girl, good girl," Tom kept saying in response to V's low growls.

A pain pill let me sleep until we were in Tom's driveway. I imagined or dreamed about Francine or someone like a sweet sister of Francine taking care of me. When Tom stopped during the eleven-hour drive, he and V didn't wake me.

Rolling out of the back seat at our destination, I had two immediate problems. "I have to hurry to the bathroom," I said, but could not hurry. I was stiff and felt a painful weight on my right foot. Then V decided to be an alpha female and positioned herself between me and anyone who tried to help me. She pretended she had never seen or smelled Tom.

"Just point, Tom. I'm desperate," I said, struggling not to hold my crotch. He opened the front door and pointed to a small half bath off the foyer. V pushed in with me.

"Bernice. We're here," Tom yelled down the long hallway. His house was U shaped, with a wide hall lining the inside of the square U. Banks of French doors opened onto a pool area on three sides. Large stones, boulders and trees defined the irregular swimming pool, creating a lush, natural looking pond view.

When I came out of the bathroom, Bernice was standing in the hall with Tom. She knelt and put her hand close to V.

"Good try, but she has to run interference for me for a little while. Sorry, she's a herder," I said to the tall, gray haired woman who knelt near me. Her hair was tied in a long pony tail and she wore a man's white shirt, silver Concho belt and faded jeans.

"Bernice Kelly, welcome." She put her hand out, but I couldn't take it. This couldn't be my Bernice, my Francine. Who was going to take care of me? This woman was a big tomboy about my age.

I leaned against the door for support. "I'm a little weak, may I go to my room?"

"If your body guard will let me, I'll take you." Bernice smiled at V and the three of us walked down the hall with an odd, bumping rhythm. Tom vanished.

The bedroom at the end of the hall was large with a couch at the foot of a queen-sized bed. The room had a masculine, library feel, but I liked it.

"Are you hungry?" Bernice asked. She gave V a wide birth, while she turned white sheets down for me. "I put extra pillows out to prop that foot on. I'll unpack after you eat something."

"Pancakes OK?" she asked before she closed the door.

"Great. Thank you." I got into the bed without any trouble. It was walking I had to get a handle on. There was a bowl of water on the floor, next to the small fireplace. Fresh cut mint mixed with small white roses sat next to a pitcher of water and a cut- glass tumbler on the night stand. Who was Tom's Bernice? She certainly wasn't Francine's sister.

I dosed until Bernice knocked softly. "Buttermilk pancakes and bacon." She placed my tray on the bed and held out a dog biscuit behind her.

The syrup was warm and the fresh orange juice cold. "This is wonderful. I didn't realize I was so hungry."

"Tom was too. I fed him first and put him to bed. He was a tired puppy," Bernice said.

"Dear heavens, he's driven for over 20 hours. How did he do it?" I said with bacon in my mouth.

"He's a driver. He'll drive when he should fly, but that's him. Now you tell me when you want to bathe. I know a trick or two about survivin' with a broken foot. Plastic bags are going to be one of your best friends."

V nuzzled her jeans pocket for another treat.

"You've had a broken foot?" I asked, trying not to talk with my mouth full of the best pancakes I'd ever tasted.

"And a broken arm, hand, and collar bone. Rodeo, barrel racing," she said, scratching V's ears. "I was mighty good, younger."

"The older I get, the better I was," I said and we laughed.

"Tell it like it is. Come on V. Don't you need to water the herb garden?" Bernice patted her thigh and gave a soft whistle, but V stayed by my bed.

I woke to V's barking. She rarely barks. Her paws pressed against the curtains separating us from the pool area. "Get down, girl. Don't tear those drapes. And don't wake Tom," I whispered. I heard a male voice with a heavy accent outside. V had heard it first. I limped to the French doors.

Bernice was talking sternly to a short, dark man in a large straw hat. "Don't come around here with that mess, Juan. I won't have it." She kicked the container of granular chlorine. "What? Did you have that left from another job and thought you would pass it off on us?"

"Don't be so hard. We all got to make some money. Even you, a little, I think." He smiled and raised his thick eyebrows. "I can bring some help for you. You work too much for him. Let's help each other."

He leaned over to pick up the chlorine. Bernice kicked him squarely in the butt and into the pool. "Last time I'm telling you. That stuff's not what we pay for. Not what we use in our environment."

"You a bitch," he yelled, climbing out of the pool.

"You a fired," Bernice mocked him. "Don't take any tools that aren't yours. You've got ten minutes." She stood with crossed arms to watch him leave.

I opened the French doors and let V run to Bernice. She paced between Juan and Bernice, as though she had been trained for this moment.

"Sorry," I said to Bernice when Juan had backed his old, red truck toward the road. "I wasn't butting in. She had to go."

"You're OK, Abby. Maybe I'll give both of you a bath," Bernice said.

"She's not a fan of bathing, but she doesn't mind a swim," I said.

Bernice walked back toward the kitchen, as though nothing had happened. Still holding a gathering basket filled with tomatoes and basil on one arm, she stooped to pick up the fifty-pound container of chlorine with the other. Her movements looked easy. She was freakishly strong. Maybe she could bathe V. after all.

We saw Tom again at seven in the evening. His face looked tired. "Long day at the salt mines. What's for dinner?" he asked.

Bernice, V and I waited for him in the kitchen. "My daddy used to say that," I said to Bernice. "I was in high school before I knew Alabama didn't have salt mines."

"Sounds like your patient is feeling better." Tom sat at the rough farm table with a groan. "Glad you're here." He patted my knee and pulled my booted foot into his lap.

V pushed herself under my propped leg. "She smells good. I guess Bernice gave her a bath. Anything that stands still long enough is going to get clean in this house." Tom said quietly, pretending to keep Bernice from hearing. He and Bernice laughed softly.

They seemed to catch a thought between them like Nelle and I sometimes do. Like my girls and I used to.

"Beef Burgundy, broccoli salad and crusty bread," Bernice said, as she opened the oven. The aroma was breath-taking.

"I talked to Nelle today. She wants you to call her tonight," Tom said, nonchalantly. He took off his coat and tie. Bernice took them without looking at him. They had a rhythm. Did he know how adamant Nelle was about me avoiding him at all costs? Why would he have made a call that I should have made?

"I didn't want her to worry," he answered the question I posed with my face.

"Who else did you call?" My voice let a little anger escape.

"Your editor. Told him you were in rehab for your foot. He needs six pages with photos in two weeks. He can send you Rick, whoever that is."

"Photographer. Did you tell him who you were?"

"Sure, Dr. Ross."

Bernice coughed a laugh from the dining room. "Come and get it," she said. The exquisite table was a photo shoot. It was a cover.

I could not stop myself from commenting. "Come and get it? We should have a butler saying dinner is served."

"We did have a butler, but Bernice fired him." Again, the two of them laughed at a private joke.

"This is the best Beef Bourguignon I've ever had." I said and touched my bread to the wine sauce that was culinary magic.

"That's what they all say," Bernice laughed with Tom, maybe because my Alabama French was out of place in this Texas house, maybe because they were or had been a couple. My heart felt like a wet, river rock.

"I have to ask. How long have you two been together? Please tell me you're not an ex-wife." I was trying to be funny and fish for answers at the same time.

"Please excuse me." Bernice put her oversized napkin on the table and left the room.

"I didn't mean to upset her. Should I try to talk to her?" I was truly sorry and wanted to suck back in the question that had jarred the peace of this house.

"Not a good idea. Bernice is sensitive about that kind of comment. She gets questions about living here a lot and it hurts her feelings. We went to school together. She runs everything for me except the law office. And once or twice she stepped in there. A few years ago, she fired a bookkeeper who was stealing. Last Summer, she turned in a paralegal who was blackmailing one of our clients. I don't know how she does it, but she does. I had to force her to hire a cleaning lady, but she only lets her work three days a week and watches her like a hawk." Tom shook his head at the puzzle that was Bernice.

"Tell me about your conversation with Nelle," I said. "By the way, Bernice has a dessert in the fridge. Just saying."

"I'll tell you in a minute. Let me check on her dessert," Tom said.

I heard him going down the hall to Bernice's suite. I half hopped, half stepped into the hallway in time to see him hand a small bowl of blackberry cobbler to her. I ducked back into the dining room before he saw me.

Our bowls of cobbler had scoops of vanilla ice cream on them. "Now, for Nelle's conversation." Tom sat down. "She thinks I'm a lying dog, not what you need, not worthy of you and thanked me for calling." He licked his spoon.

"What if she tells the girls where I am. They'll call her when they finally discover I'm MIA." I finished my dessert.

"Is everything she cooks this good?" I asked.

"Pretty much. It's what she does, besides ride." He took our plates and bowls to the kitchen sink. "I told Nelle about your daughters not picking you up at the hospital or offering to help you at home for a few days. She was furious. Called them names she had called me a few minutes earlier. I promised her not to do anything but take care of you until she gets here."

"She's coming here?" I tried to stand up, forgot about my foot and plopped back into a dining chair.

"I'll fly her out at the end of the week. I thought you would feel more comfortable with her here."

"Oh, Tom Ross, I love you. I mean, thank you so much for understanding." What is wrong with me? I can't take any more pain pills.

"Maybe you can fly back with her, if you're unhappy here or want to go back to work." He sounded really tired now. The long drives and Judge Moreno had taken their toll.

"We both need to get some rest," he said in his lowest bass range. Did he know what that voice did to me? He kissed me on my cheek, then on my mouth. "Yep, I could get used to you," he said. "Good night."

I stood in the same spot a long time. V came from the bedroom and herded me to bed. "OK, I'll just take one more pain pill," I said to V. "You know they make me stupid."

Bernice woke me with a quiet knock. "You up?" She opened the door, then let V out. "You want to eat in here or the kitchen?" She showed no hostility or awkwardness from the night before.

"I'm not dressed," I stammered.

"Tom's already left for work. And I'm riding this morning. What'll it be?"

"Please don't go to any trouble."

"Too late," she laughed.

"Kitchen. Let me get my robe. Where do you ride? Is it nearby? Where do you keep your horse?" I was still sleepy and slipped my robe on wrong side out. We laughed together. We sounded like a pair, like Tom and Bernice or Nelle and me. I had gotten over my initial disappointment at Bernice not being like Francine. Now, I wanted her as a friend. Maybe we both needed a friend.

"There's a good stable about a mile from here. I've had Lucky there about five years. We won a lot of events together, but he's like me, getting old. We still ride a little, so neither of us gets too sad."

I followed her to the kitchen. She spooned scrambled eggs, salsa and crispy bacon on tortillas, rolled them and garnished with sour cream. "Instant breakfast," she said.

"Tom keeps two stalls for me, so I bought Sundance two years ago. He's a looker and rides like a rocking chair."

"Tom has stalls, but no horses?"

"He knows me. I can't be happy without a horse somewhere. I don't compete anymore, but it's in my blood. Just hanging around the stable and smelling that good horse and hay smell lowers my blood pressure."

"Tom says you two went to school together." I still felt there was more between them, maybe high school crush, some bond.

"We three went to school together. It was always a threesome." She leaned her head back and smiled. My brother was Tom's best friend. Mine, too. He was something. Sorry." Bernice wiped her eyes with the back of her hand. "Guess I'll never get over losing him."

"Better ride my bad boys before they get too sassy to put a saddle on. Chicken salad in the fridge for lunch. Rest." She jogged out the side door where she parked her white Jeep. She had a box of sliced apples and sweet potatoes for her bad boys.

I welcomed time alone in Tom's rambling house. An idea washed over me. I retrieved my camera from my carry-on luggage and set the dining table just as Bernice had. I took twenty photos, copying some of the angles I had seen Rick use. I began to write copy for the pictures that I hoped were usable. I referenced china patterns, linen manufacturers, silver styles and marks, then called Fed Ex for a pick up. I had enough material for a two-page article. Now I needed only one more brainstorm.

I walked carefully into the kitchen for chicken salad and there it was. There it was! The pool. Tomorrow I would get more film and write about the lush pond, the garden focal point that was a swimming pool. I was responsible for three articles a month to keep my job. More talented people were lined up to work on our magazine staff. Some of the younger writers were willing to work free for the experience. It was important to safeguard my position.

Chapter Twenty-eight

HIDE AND WATCH

I called Ida at the magazine office to give her a heads up about the articles.

"Let me give you a heads up," she said, then started to whisper. LeeAnn, you know, from my camping group, works for a survey company. Told me all the property around your Tennessee River house is being surveyed by a big hotel and resort group out of Texas."

"What does that mean to me?" I didn't recognize the threat that made Ida whisper.

"Wait, there's more. Guess what company is doing all the paper work, real estate contracts and insurance policies for the investors? Claude Copenhaven. Bastard."

"Please let me show you to the conference room. Mr. Wheaton will meet with you shortly. Please serve yourself coffee."

Ida shifted her voice back to a whisper. "LeeAnn said she heard that he told the investors not to worry about that little six acres in the center, that his daughters actually owned it and he would arrange for them sell it to him."

"That doesn't make sense. Why would they think they own the property? I mean, I'll leave it to them, but. . ." I remembered Sarah's tirade about the car and the River Cottage when I called from the hospital.

"Ida, I know the girls aren't in on this. If they were, he wouldn't have asked me to sell it to him."

"But you said no. I think you said there's not that much money. Get out."

"You are the worst eaves dropper."

"Or the best. Want to hear more? Sara has called here five times, trying to find out how to get in touch with you. I just played dumb. She knew what I was doing and I don't care." Ida interrupted her whispers. "Please be seated. Our photographer will be here in a few minutes. He is finishing a shoot in Mountain Brook and your appointment is not until eleven."

"Another designer who wants an article written about her latest project. I think it's just her own house. Everybody's a designer, now. Anyway, Lee Ann's boss, with whom she has a date, Friday, by the way, said the Corps of Engineers won't approve a tract of land for a resort without the limestone bluff behind your cottage being included."

"It would cost millions to level that bluff to build on, I said. "We bought that six acres behind the cottage just to have easy access around the bluff to the house from the old highway. I think your friend has the wrong information."

"She is me at the surveying company. She hears everything. Trust me. Old Claude is trying to pull a fast one. More, Lee Ann saw an artist rendering for the investors showing the main building on top of the bluff. The name of the development is Overlook."

"Ida, you are a genius. I wouldn't sell it now for a million dollars."

"I hope not. The investment group, the developers call them The Texas Outlaws, is willing to pay twelve million, according to Katie Allen at First Federal. But you didn't hear that from me."

That had been the yellow note's warning. I had missed it.

"Is there, like, a female mafia? I mean this is big and silent."

"Katie said the bank has to have a done deal before they can pull environmental permits. Your ex has promised to have the six-acre parcel secured."

"I need to make a couple of phone calls. Call you back in an hour. Hey Ida, Thanks."

I could not call Nelle's number fast enough. "Nelle, Nelle, you can't believe what that son of a bitch has done."

"I knew it, after all that talk about you on the phone."

"No, Nelle, the other son of a bitch, Claude."

After briefing her on the threat to my little river cottage and the millions of dollars to be made by owning a worthless limestone bluff on the Tennessee River, I asked her advice on the hardest part of the dilemma, my daughters.

"They can't be a part of this. They will inherit everything I have. They would never trick me or cheat me." My voice was almost begging Nelle to agree.

"Not knowingly, but their father can be persuasive. And a big lump of money would change their lives. When you're young, an inheritance seems light years away. Of course, I'm sure they would never know he had gotten the lion's share. And you know he would."

"What can I do?" My foot was hurting again and I was angry and weepy at the same time. Poor, pitiful me. "Stop being a victim, girl." My brain shouted. I was glad Bernice was not here to see me.

"I wouldn't have said this before you were left in the hospital waiting room, but here goes," Nelle paused. She knew the inherent danger of speaking negatively about someone's child. "Hide and watch. If one comes to you with a proposition to inherit the house early, set up a family trust, or asks you to sell it to them and just use it as long as you want to, hide and watch. If one says my boy-friend just came into some money and wants to buy it from you as our first home, you will know. As painful as it may be, you have to hide and watch. Do not appear to have any knowledge of The Overlook. I've said too much, but you asked me."

"I trust you Nelle, that's why I called. By the way, Tom is being wonderful and his housekeeper, Bernice, old friend, best cook in the world, is wonderful, too. Can't wait for you to get to know them. Your instincts are better than mine, but I think we are OK. Love you."

I decided not to share the river cottage saga with Tom. He had a lot going on and I must seem like a walking soap opera, already.

He and Bernice came home about the same time. Both worn out. "Pizza tonight?" Bernice asked Tom.

"With a big salad?" he asked, pulling off his coat and tie.

"You got it." She automatically took his things. "I need a shower first," she said.

"Want a drink?" Tom said.

"Sure," Bernice and I said together.

"Coming up." Tom went to the kitchen for ice. I followed him clumsily.

"I wanted to ask you about Bernice's brother. She was so sad this morning. She said she would never get over losing him."

"Neither of us will. He was part of us, the best part. Bernard was always the leader, even when we were children. But it's been harder for Bernice. She never married, never really dated. I guess we were all she needed, and her horses. They were twins, you know."

"Oh, Tom. Tom, how awful. I didn't know." I leaned on him. "That breaks my heart."

"I'll take her a gin and tonic, for when she gets out of the shower." He walked away from me, down the long hall.

The phone rang. "For you, Abby." Tom called from the hallway. I sat on a kitchen stool and talked to my oldest daughter on a wall phone.

Sara apologized for not coming to the hospital and for hanging up on me about using my car while I was unable to drive. "I was so overwhelmed, I just took it out on you, Mother," she said. "I love you."

"I was overwhelmed, too, Sara. In fact, I was almost helpless for a little while. It was a frightening feeling. But I'm over it."

"Good news," she said. I'm engaged. Ken asked me Saturday night. I thought Daddy had already talked to you about buying the river cottage for us as a wedding present. He told me you said no, no matter how much money he was willing to pay. But yesterday, Daddy said he wasn't sure you knew it was for me. That you got mad about his girl-friend's family using it, or something. You know he's not the best communicator in the world." She gave me a silly, surface laugh, which didn't sound like her.

"I don't understand this young man I've never met, not being able to afford a car, but now, he wants to own the river cottage. Has he ever seen it?" I said calmly. Nelle was right. It was painful to hide and watch.

"Is there someone with you? Is it just the two of us talking, like we used to?"

"No, Mother, Daddy's here. He really wants to do this." She was crying.

"I'm sure he does. Let me think about it. When will I meet your young man? Have you thought about a date?"

"I don't know, Mother. It's kind of sudden. You know, it may not actually happen."

"I love you. Remember that. What about your sister? She's close enough in Nashville to enjoy the cottage more than you in Atlanta. Maybe she wants ownership, too. You and your father think about that, while you decide what to do with my property."

I faintly heard a male voice in the background say, "She knows something's up."

Sara did not call again. Millicent never mentioned the cottage when checking on me.

I called Katie Allen at First Federal bright and early. I asked if she worked on commission and if so, could I retain her services to draw up a contract with the Overlook Investment Group. I gave Ida Cummings as my reference and contact person. Katie understood.

"I think I can have an offer for you in the morning," she said.

"Please make sure Lee Ann at Surveys, Inc. has a fee listed in the contract, perhaps one percent."

I called Nelle to tell her hide and watch worked. It worked to the tune of eleven million dollars.

Chapter Twenty-nine

GIRLS RULE

I dreamed about the coolness of the pool water. I wondered how I could get my ball and chain boot off. The tight boot dominated every move. My hip and back were stiff with lugging the ugly thing around. A soak in the dark pool appealed to me, but Bernice and Tom would object to removing the boot. I knew I could relax and be careful not to move or injure my foot. The swelling had gone down. I slipped off the boot's Velcro straps and floated in a blind corner of the pool. A large boulder blocked my shallow location from the glass doors of the house, where I had exited unseen. Without the pool area lighting, I could soak, invisible to the world. I almost dozed off. Then V started barking a strange, rapid bark.

She had pushed the French doors of my room open to follow me and now ran up and down the stone deck, barking wildly. "Hush. You're going to wake everybody in the house up. Come here, girl." No response, just loud, incessant barking. Then I saw the source of her hysteria. Two men hurried out of the kitchen door and ran toward the garage. V blocked their way, so they turned toward a side gate leading to the front yard. V jumped at them and growled in a way I had never heard. She kept a line between the pool and the house, cutting off any retreat the intruders might have.

"Juan, grab that pole and knock her off. We got to get out of here." The larger man said.

A pool net on a long metal pole became Juan's weapon. He hit V on the first swing. She didn't make a sound, but crouched for a jump at his head on his next swing. I couldn't get out of the water to help her. The men had not seen me until I threw a stone from the edge of the pool, barely missing the man with the pole. Both men looked at the pool. I could not move. "They are going to kill me and my dog," I whispered.

Suddenly all the lights in the pool area came on. The whole back yard and grounds were washed in bright light. "Don't move a muscle. Drop that pole." Bernice, in her red robe, held the biggest pistol I had ever seen. She was smiling.

"Did you forget something, Juan? What's in your pockets?" Bernice gestured with the gun. "Let me see."

Like a child caught in the act, Juan pulled a pistol and a small jewelry box from his jacket.

"Put everything on the ground," Bernice said.

"Good thing you didn't hurt that dog. We wouldn't be waitin' for the police. Don't even think about running. This thing won't just shoot you in the leg, it'll blow your leg off. Try me."

V stopped barking and paced back and forth between the pool and the men. I think she and Bernice wanted them to run.

"Juan, I told you not to bring your mess around here. Now you brought it all. Who's this fella with you?"

"My cousin, Bubba."

"We was jus gettin' our stuff, man," Bubba said.

"Show and tell, Bubba," Bernice pointed the barrel at his head.

He opened his jacket and held a cloth bag out. Without being told, he placed the heavy bag filled with silver on the ground.

"We may find some more stuff that doesn't belong to you when the police get here," Bernice said. She was not afraid or nervous. She was enjoying her role.

From my low vantage point, I could see their bulging pants and jackets, too warm for summer, but just right for carrying out loot.

The police arrived six minutes before Tom. Tom's friend with a police scanner had alerted him.

A young, Black policeman tried to pull me onto the stone deck. It hurt to move. How did I think I was going to get out? "Please, give me a minute. I'm injured."

He jumped in the shallow water and waded toward me, shoes, uniform and all. "Are you shot, ma'am?"

"No, no, I'm sorry. I have a fractured foot."

"How do you know? He asked, as patiently as a nurse in an old folks' home.

"A doctor told me so in Birmingham, last week," I said quietly.

He splashed out of the water muttering angrily. "Damn Alabama crazies!"

Only when Tom got home did I feel safe enough to get out of the water. He helped me stand and then wrapped a towel around me, while Bernice spoke to the police.

"Bernice is a rock star. You should have seen her! Give that girl a raise." I was excited. I wanted to dance on the stone pavers, sing *Twist and Shout*, kiss Tom Ross. I had done nothing, but felt like a heroine.

"She makes more than I do now. Let's get you off that foot."

Bernice joined us. I saw you in the pool. What's wrong with you? V could have been hurt." She turned to Tom. "Sorry I didn't shoot them, but I couldn't find my lawyer to see what my rights were."

Tom and Bernice embraced. "God, he would be proud of you, girl."

"I threw a rock at them," I said weakly. Suddenly I felt dizzy.

"Put her to bed for me, she's shaking." Bernice said and touched me on the shoulder. "Don't take that boot off again."

She was right. The cool water and freedom from the heavy boot felt wonderful, but now my ankle and arch were throbbing. The pressure of climbing out of the shallows had re-injured my foot.

I leaned on Tom like a crutch and winced. "Stop. It hurts too much."

He picked me up, bride fashion. "Glad we don't have to go far," he said.

"Are you showing off for Bernice?" I said. I knew I was too heavy for him. We were close to the same size.

"You know she could carry you better than I can. But I'm trying to hold on to a little pride." He was breathing heavily when he put me on the bed.

"Here's another towel. Where are some dry pajamas?" he panted.

"Tom, lie down by me for a minute." He did and we held each other without talking. I think we fell asleep, damp towels around us.

I woke myself with a snort of a snore. Tom was still asleep. I carefully removed the towels that entangled us and kissed his face. He had a citrus smell that made me want to keep my face next to his for the rest of the night, maybe forever.

I started to roll over on this delicious, sleeping man, so warm in my bed, but the stupid boot slapped the romance away with a sharp pain. How much could I do without waking him. Why did I continue to play games, keep odd scores? Gently, I rubbed under his shirt and then, his pants. Just feeling his boxer shorts excited me. I wanted to touch him, but needed him to stay asleep.

I put my lips on his and gently rubbed, without kissing. The sensation of dry, smooth lips on lips was thrilling. "Please don't wake up," I whispered. Moving inch at a time, I undressed Tom Ross in my bed. "What is wrong with you?" I said to myself. You will die if he wakes up. You know he will wake up.

"Mind, how you do go on." I said or thought. I was taking short, shallow breaths and was not sure this was happening.

It took twenty minutes, but he was naked in my bed. He had not stirred. I ran my hands over his body, from chest to feet. I delicately touched his hands and the hard, silky object between his legs. "Please stay asleep," I said with my lips touching his ear.

I untied my robe and worked out of the wet night shirt I had worn in the pool. I rolled onto him with more success, this time, carefully not moving the boot at all.

Tom Ross woke up. The slow, gentle love making that followed made me climax twice before he did. "What's wrong with me?"

We fell asleep again, touching, but not talking.

I awoke to a bright morning, almost nine o'clock. My boot was in place, now, over a man's white sock. A blue and white Chinese robe wrapped my nude body. "Dear God, he has seen me naked and knows I'm crazy," I whispered. V greeted me in the hall on my hobble to the kitchen for coffee.

"Where have you been, big girl?" I rubbed her head and sat in a chair pulled out from the old farm table.

"She bunked with me last night. I was surprised she stayed," Bernice said, pouring coffee in a white mug for me. "How did you sleep? I know that was scary out by the pool."

Did she know? "I slept really well." I sipped my coffee. She already knew the right amount of cream to add.

"We need to talk," Bernice said, sitting across from me at the table. She knows. She held her mug in both hands, not looking at me.

"If you and Tom live here at some point, do I stay or go? Sorry, I'm not good at beating around the bush," Bernice said.

"First, Tom has not asked me to marry him," I answered primly.

"I didn't say marry," Bernice smiled. She knew.

"You were here first. I guess you sort of have dibs, from way back. I like you being here. Your strength is contagious, so is your energy. Tom loves you and I want to be your friend. I feel safe with you and Tom."

We toasted coffee mugs. "I know we don't have much, besides Tom, in common, but we can make it work," Bernice said. Her sigh sounded relieved, when she stood up to cook breakfast. We had waffles, strawberries and whipped cream with slivered almonds.

"Have you ever been to a beauty pageant?" I asked.

"Not going to happen," Bernice said with her back to me. "You're a judge and I'm a judge not."

"Maybe we can write a country song together," I said. And we did.

Ann Miller Hopkins presents her first novel, inspired by a large family of strong, funny, beautiful women. Originally from Alabama, she now lives with her husband in Blue Mountain Beach, Florida.

Hopkins' first novel, *Judge Not,* is *laugh out loud and weep silently good fiction. Abby is a middle-aged, ex-beauty queen judging on the pageant circuit. She is hilarious juggling sarcastic observations, old friendships and crazy romantic adventures.*

You will remember the women and wisdom in this fast read long after you put the book down.

A second novel, **The Cousins**, *follows this Summer.*